I0602331

PERSEPHONE

CS-405: BOOK THREE

BLAZE WARD

KNOTTED ROAD PRESS

Persephone
CS-405: Book Three
Blaze Ward
Copyright © 2019 Blaze Ward
All rights reserved
Published by Knotted Road Press
www.KnottedRoadPress.com

ISBN: 978-1-64470-029-7

Cover art:

ID 52628760 © Elena Polina | Dreamstime.com
ID 39495850 © Algol | Dreamstime.com

Cover and interior design © 2019 Knotted Road Press

Never miss a release!
If you'd like to be notified of new releases, sign up for my newsletter.

I only send out newsletters once a quarter, will never spam you, or use your email for nefarious purposes. You can also unsubscribe at any time.

http://www.blazeward.com/newsletter/

This book is licensed for your personal enjoyment only. All rights reserved. This is a work of fiction. All characters and events portrayed in this book are fictional, and any resemblance to real people or incidents is purely coincidental. This book, or parts thereof, may not be reproduced in any form without permission.

ALSO BY BLAZE WARD

The Jessica Keller Chronicles

Auberon

Queen of the Pirates

Last of the Immortals

Goddess of War

Flight of the Blackbird

The Red Admiral

St. Legier

CS-405

Queen Anne's Revenge

Packmule

Persephone

Additional Alexandria Station Stories

The Story Road

Siren

Two Bottles of Wine with a War God

The Science Officer Series

The Science Officer

The Mind Field

The Gilded Cage

The Pleasure Dome

The Doomsday Vault

The Last Flagship

The Hammerfield Gambit

The Hammerfield Payoff

Doyle Iwakuma Stories

The Librarian

Demigod

Greater Than The Gods Intended

Other Science Fiction Stories

Myrmidons

Moonshot

Menelaus

Earthquake Gun

Moscow Gold

Fairchild

White Crane

***The Collective* Universe**

The Shipwrecked Mermaid

Imposters

LIGHTHOUSE STATION (NOVEMBER 1, 402)

THEIR CHARTS CALLED it *Lighthouse Station*, but newly-minted *RAN* Centurion Granville Veitengruber thought of it using the designation the *Fribourg* Fleet would have used: *Forward Base Battenhouse*, named for the first commanding officer, *CS-405*'s former and now semi-retired Boatswain, Bok Battenhouse.

CS-405 was above Granville's ship in orbit, Admiral Kosnett protecting the flock of stolen vessels against sudden surprises. *RAN Packmule*, the stolen mega-freighter that was their mobile larder, was down lower, where her three shuttles could make faster flights in both directions with cargo containers. *RAN Queen Anne's Revenge*, the cargo ship borrowed temporarily from Kiel and Lan, was already in her descent to the planet.

Kosnett had repeatedly made it clear that they would be returning the vessel to its rightful owners at some future point. Or replacing it if they were unable.

"*405*, this is *Persephone*," Granville said into the microphone. "Beginning our descent now."

He was in command of the fourth vessel, comprised of two C-class hulls, *C-4268* and *C-4711* that they had stolen and reassembled on *Mansi-D* into a single warship, *Persephone*.

The four vessels, plus the three shuttles from *Packmule*, were configured to talk via tight-beam lasers these days, rather than encoded radio signals. It let them move silently while stalking their prey, since even the slightest detection of a transmission might give too much away.

The return message from the flagship was a standard message, rather than a longer message, but it still warmed his heart. It was what would have come from the Imperial Admiral commanding, had this been a *Fribourger* squadron, and not *Aquitaine*.

Godspeed.

Nothing more.

CS-405 would be deploying their administrative shuttle to bring the Admiral and his temporary First Officer down to the ground shortly, as would *Packmule*, with the insertion shuttle *Saddlebags* bringing Captain Lau and Centurion Doctor Gave as well.

It was a Council of War, but it would be done on the ground, rather than aboard the flagship, on an anciently-terraformed planet that *Buran* had never gotten around to colonizing, so Admiral Kosnett had done it instead. If they were to be pirates, and they thought of themselves that way, then nothing was going to be done by halves.

That included Granville making his first landfall in a

stolen and salvaged warship that had once belonged to the *Fribourg Empire*, before vanishing from history more than a decade ago.

They were both coming home.

CATTLE RANCH (NOVEMBER 2, 402)

HEATHER WAS SIMPLY amazed at how much work had been completed in the time they had been gone to *Mansi*. More fences were up, with small turrets added in several places, presumably tracking predators wanting to bother the cattle or chickens that now called *Lighthouse Station* home.

She stood on the front porch facing west. From here, she looked up the hill to the closest cattle pen, and beyond that, the ring of mountains that sealed this valley off from the rest of the planet. Downhill, the slope slowly faded down into the massive lake that sat at the bottom of the valley.

In front of her, Bok had leveled a massive-enough space that they had been able to put all the vessels down at once: Phil's admin shuttle, her insertion shuttle, Siobhan's freighter, and Veitengruber's cutter.

All those ships. They had started in April with just *CS-405*, and it was only November.

"Hey," Siobhan suddenly stuck her head out the front door and barked. "Phil's ready. Wanna get your butt in motion?"

"Coming," Heather replied, turning to follow *Lady Blackbeard* into the front room.

When they built this place, the crew had thrown together a quick frame for a house. Two stories and big enough for the four people on permanent assignment to each have their own room. It was also big enough that thirty more could stay here, lacking only enough bathrooms and water heaters for a mob like that.

Instead of a traditional salon, the front door opened onto an Operations Center, such as it was. Rough-hewn tables one meter by three on two sides of the room. Every spare chair that they had been able to break out of storage on *405* or steal along the way looked like a bizarrely-mismatched flock of ugly seagulls. Maps were tacked to walls and strewn on the table where Phil was holding court with a mug of fresh tea in one hand, made from the first batch of leaves cut and dried on *Lighthouse Station* by First-Rate-Spacer Shelby Flud.

They had even located something vaguely equivalent to maple trees in the nearby forest, except these had sap that ran all year long, however slowly, so they had tapped them for a sweetener syrup. Crazy, redneck homesteaders, the lot of them.

She took the empty chair next to Veitengruber and measured faces. He didn't even have a proper First Officer yet. Hell, his whole crew right now was just two engineers: Galin Tuason and Isiah Olshefski, although he would pick up some gunners in a few days.

Bok was here as base commander. Phil and Evan, representing both *CS-405* and squadron command. *Lady Blackbeard* and *Stunt Dude*, also occasionally known as Siobhan Skokomish and Trinidad Mildon. Her and Andre, with him looking more like a line officer and less like a nurse these days. He might even come to like being in command, but she wasn't going to tell him that.

Phil rapped his knuckles on the table to get everyone to settle down.

"Okay," he said simply. "We've done the crazy, the stupid, and the impossible. So far. We've established a base behind enemy lines. We've stolen a sector supply vessel, a scout, and a pocket warship. The black flag is hopefully inspiring a wave of terror over these two sectors, to the point that Jessica will find them softened up when she comes back, hopefully with a second Imperial fleet to kick some ass. Is it enough? The table is open for discussion. Nothing leaves this room."

He nodded, looking more like a presiding judge than a commanding officer, but Heather supposed he was acting the role of a Fleet Centurion these days. Or an Imperial Admiral of the White. She grinned at that thought.

"Heather?" he asked, staring fiercely back at her.

"Can we legitimately call ourselves Second Expeditionary Fleet?" she asked.

"Stop reading my mind!" Siobhan mock-challenged her from across the table with a laugh.

They had spent too much time together, originally as First and Second Officers under Phil, and now as breveted Command Centurions with their own ships in Phil's squadron.

"We may not," Phil intoned severely. "The Senate has not authorized a new command, nor established a base for it. I am willing to usurp the First Lord as far as we've gone, but not the civilians above her."

"Awwwww," Siobhan sulked.

Heather had to agree. It was a fine point, but this was all about the legalisms by now. They could have, possibly *should have* gone home as soon as they had enough food to make the journey safely. Instead, they had expanded their war.

Everyone at this table would face a Court Martial when they got home. Probably something along the lines of *Unlawfully Absent*, since no navy lawyer was ever going to be able to make *Cowardice in the Face of the Enemy* stick on this group.

Phil's career might be over. Hell, all their careers might be over. At least as long as it took for them to find the Imperial Ambassador and enlist under Karl VIII. She'd take them all in a heartbeat.

"Sir? If I may?" Granville spoke up from next to her.

His voice wasn't diffident. He had gotten over the slave persona fairly quickly, but there also wasn't the fire and craziness you would expect from a former fighter jock.

Phil nodded.

"Perhaps Seventeenth Imperial Police Protectorate would be more appropriate?" Granville offered. "The cutter *C-4711*, which provided the bow section of my vessel, was assigned to that squadron when it was taken eleven years ago."

"I believe we're a little past customs patrols and Search

and Rescue, but I will take it under advisement, Centurion," Phil noted with a smile.

Veitengruber nodded and leaned back. Heather smiled in his direction. He was fitting in with the group, remembering what it meant to be an officer in a formal navy. And he was a good man.

"*Mansi-B,*" *Stunt Dude* spoke up, turning the conversation back to the original topic. "We're only going to get one clean chance at it. Do we risk everything, or go home and bring in a full strike fleet? Do we have enough guns now? We've got crazy."

"Station like that doesn't have Primaries," Bok replied in a quiet drawl. "You'll be facing Fours and missiles. Probably not a lot of overlap on the guns, but they'll throw darts at you all day."

"And we're an escort specifically designed to engage that sort of threat," Evan leaned into the conversation. "Plus *Persephone* has guns. If they don't have a resupply capacity handy, they'll have to run out at some point."

"Evan, plot me an overlap map of the big guns when we get back to the ship," Phil ordered, glancing to one side of the table. "Assume our Type-4 beam and add three percent, just to humor me."

"Yes, sir."

"Now, all this talk of assaulting the planet is moot, unless one of you can explain to me how we punch a hole in their defensive net in the first place," Phil continued.

"Pull a Kigali," Heather offered in a flat, humorless tone. While laughing inside.

The room erupted with conversations at her words,

which she had expected. Phil actually had to raise his voice to finally get everyone else to shut up.

"Okay, Heather," Phil said. "What would our crazed *Navigator* of an Escort Team Commander do here?"

"He might make a high-speed run at the station in JumpSpace," she replied. "Ride it all the way in until the edge of the gravity well kicked him out, and then open up on the station with everything he had."

"We're an escort, Heather," Phil said. "Even a splash of Type-1-Pulse beams aren't going to do that much damage, and then you're racing full tilt at one of the other stations, who will see you coming, and not be able to Jump clear because your Matrix has collapsed and you have to rebuild it."

"Not if you're going straight down, Phil," she smiled, turning to Granville next to her. "*Persephone* can land, and I'm betting none of the other stations will be able to range on her from orbit."

"They'll still have missiles," Siobhan spoke up half-heartedly.

"Through an atmosphere at a moving target?" Heather laughed. "Please do. Every bird you waste firing down is one fewer that you can't replace later."

"How does *Persephone* kill a station on a fencing pass?" Phil asked.

Heather started to speak, but closed her mouth when Granville suddenly leaned forward and put his hand on the table.

"With a bloody lot of missiles in single-shot, launch tubes around the outside of my hull," he smiled cruelly.

"Fired simultaneously with us achieving our first weapons lock."

"Did you two already work this out?" Siobhan sulked. "Are you leaving me out of all the fun, now?"

"No," Heather replied. "This was a conversation we had back on *Mansi-D*. Filling up the containers on *Caravan* with a bunch of missiles, flying up to a station like we had a food delivery, and killing the place point-blank when they lowered their shields for docking."

"Will it work?" Phil asked.

Heather shrugged, and caught Granville doing the same out of the corner of her eye.

"We'd need Kam and her crew," she said. "But I'd tell them it was impossible. Maybe even bet them money on the topic and have them prove me wrong."

The whole table laughed.

Never tell an engineer something can't be done. Unless you want to awaken the technological beast from his torpid slumber.

"What about me?" Siobhan's voice had gone almost plaintive.

"You're a unicorn," Heather grinned.

"A what?"

"A pretty horse with a magical horn in the middle of its forehead," she continued.

"Still not seeing it."

"We stole that other forward section at *Mansi-D*," she said. "The front third of *C-4268* that had been killed. It has a Type-3 beam mount that we salvaged in orbit."

"Did you just get evil?" Siobhan asked, her head

turning a little sideways so she could give off some polite side-eye.

"Maybe," Heather agreed. "Wanna tell Markus Dunklin that there's no way in hell he could mount it inside *Anna's* forward bay and wire up enough generators and batteries that you could fire it and not cook your electronics?"

"Yup, evil," Siobhan agreed. "Why?"

"Because there is still a kremlin on the surface of *Mansi-B*," Phil interjected. "I would include a reasonable planetary shield overhead to protect me from orbital bombardments, just in case."

"Bingo," Heather supplied. "Those are horizontal. What happens when you're below them, coming up at him from the side and firing a Type-3 into his butt? Plus *Persephone* doing the same from another flank?"

"Weasels in the chicken coop," Bok said. "Lost two here that way, until I tuned the pulse turret on top to kill anything that small it saw inside the wire that wasn't a chicken. Sorry about the bunnies. Got rid of the mole problem, though."

More laughter. Bok was sixty-two years Standard, and had been on Active Duty for more than forty of those, but in the last few months had reverted to the rancher kid from five decades ago, complete with drawl.

"Okay, so we think we could kill the command station overhead," Phil said. "Heather, work with Evan and whoever else you need to put together a feasibility study. We still do not know how many men are down there that need rescuing, and I'm not about to presume that one of those dead frigates or cruisers we saw in orbit will work, so we need transport to get as many home as we can. This is why I asked if we go home to get help."

"We could steal a cruise ship," Andre Gave, the nurse-turned-pirate asked, a broad, crazy smile on his face suddenly.

The whole room fell to stunned silence.

"What?" he demanded sarcastically. "Just because I took a Hippocratic Oath doesn't mean I can't pirate with you people."

"Where do we get a cruise ship?" *Stunt Dude* asked.

"How the hell should I know?" Andre fired back. "Go ask Lan and Kiel, maybe."

Heather started to laugh. They all did.

But then they stopped. Hard silence.

Phil had that look on his face.

Shit, they really were going to, weren't they?

THE SHUTTLE HAD DEPOSITED them in the middle of an obvious landing field, on the surface of the new, secret base deep inside *The Holding*. It was early morning, local time, with the sun just coming over the eastern peaks and a fog still burning off on the lake below them on the hillside.

Lan recognized *Resolute Revolution*, sitting with several other vessels. Director Kosnett's team had rechristened her *Queen Anne's Revenge* after some ancient pirate ship from Earth. She looked to be in better condition than the vessel had been when he and Kiel first purchased it, the benefit of having an entire crew of trained experts dedicated to keeping it in top shape.

Secretly, Lan was torn. On the one hand, Director Kosnett had promised to return the vessel and make them whole in the legal sense, providing an equivalent cargo for the one he had stolen.

On the other hand, it might be interesting if the man

had to buy them a newer vessel, done up in the style of the *Fribourg* barbarians. They had certain technological edges that *The Eldest* had not pursued because his *Sentient* ships were good enough. But a ship that didn't need to drop out of JumpSpace except at its target would save tremendous time for them as a commercial venture, allowing them to move between markets so much faster.

Perhaps he could get a contract hauling mail and priority shipments between worlds and charge an extra premium?

But that wasn't why they had asked him and his spouse to join them down on the surface of the new world.

And he had asked. Director Kosnett could have easily ordered them to attend him. Forced them into the administrative shuttle without an explanation. Instead, he had sent a crewman to deliver a hand-written letter.

Lan hadn't been on the surface of a planet in nearly two years. He and Kiel normally ran between stations in orbit, only landing on worlds not serviced by a useful station. It felt weird.

Lighthouse Station was the name the barbarians had chosen. Lan had no idea where they actually were, in relation to any other planet, which was just as well. He couldn't be accused of anything later. And how did anyone expect a forty-four-year-old man and his forty-seven-year-old wife to overcome an entire warship filled with armed pirates?

Lan scanned the coops and pastures around them, letting the smell on the morning breeze welcome him. Cow shit. And chicken shit. It reminded him of his youth, and the reasons he had wanted to serve on a spaceship in the first place.

He laughed to himself as Kiel took his hand, an eyebrow raised.

"Cows," he said, as if that explained everything.

Maybe it did. They were no more native to this world than he was. Both the product of competent pirates with a decided sense of humor.

"Moo," she giggled back.

They weren't even under guard, as they approached the newly-built house. Merely escorted by one of the female marines that made up part of his normal bodyguard.

That was how Lan had taken to thinking of them.

Inside the building, a crowd had taken over the main room, with two big tables slid together and lots of mismatched chairs. *Resolute Revolution* had nothing but seats fixed to bulkheads and flip-down jumpseats, so these had been stolen from someone else.

Director Kosnett rose and bowed lightly to them, a proper Khan recognizing honored guests to his Court. Lan's smile spread and he bowed back even deeper.

These barbarians were such interesting and polite people for murderous bastards coming to snatch a six-year-old Lan from his dormitory for being naughty. Or something like that.

They were seated next to the Director, across from two other sub-commanders: *Lady Blackbeard* Skokomish, and *Ground Control* Lau, according to the stories he and his spouse had picked up third-hand from their marine escorts and others in the wardroom for dinner. Many of the others were recurring characters in Kosnett's drama, actors with pay-for-play contracts who came and went as the chess master moved his pieces around the board.

"Thank you for joining us," Director Kosnett said. "My crew of lunatic pirates might have finally dreamed up the impossible, and someone suggested that the two of you might be able to offer interesting suggestions."

"Indeed?" Kiel spoke.

She always spoke for them, as a rule. He would trust her judgment in all things, as the only bad decision the woman had ever made was marrying him.

"And, at the very least, there will be fresh eggs and homemade cheese omelets, with beef bacon and fresh vegetables from the greenhouse," Kosnett continued.

Lan felt his eyes grow wide. Fresh omelets, but that made sense, as they had captured chickens, as well as cattle. This was turning into a proper ranch.

Where in the galaxy did these barbarians get the people to do all this?

"Ask, Director Kosnett," Kiel smiled. "We will aid you as our consciences allow."

"We have, to date, stolen three vessels from *The Holding*," he said, referring to *Resolute Revolution*, the food transport now called *Packmule*, and the new escort he had previously heard mentioned. They had seen it on landing, parked across the yard, an older Imperial ship that they had apparently snuck out from under the noses of the guards, to hear his marines snicker.

"Our next mission is an entire order of magnitude larger and more dangerous than anything we have attempted," Kosnett explained.

"Okay," Kiel said carefully.

"We believe we have located the planet *Mansi*," Kosnett said. "Based on Lan's remembrances and our own field observations."

"Truly?" Lan gasped. "The prison world?"

"We think so," Kosnett said. "We have two options now."

Rather than continue, Kosnett turned to his First Officer, the woman known now as *Ground Control*, for reasons that had not been explained any more adequately than had the nickname for the Chief of Security who was universally *Stunt Dude*.

The woman gestured to another person and a projection took shape between them, hovering over the table. Eight stations were marked with stars, in a rigid box defending all approaches to an unknown planet.

Lan felt the ghost rise up from deep within his soul as the memories came back.

"This is *Mansi-B*," she began. "We scanned the planet extensively but passively from the shadows of *Mansi-D*, and have identified the station we believe is the palace of the Khan."

One of the station in the northern hemisphere changed from red to white.

"We believe we can disable or destroy this station," the woman continued in a hard, angry voice. "That opens a path to the surface, where we would destroy the kremlin on the ground. At that point, we could rescue any and possibly all of the prisoners currently being held."

"But?" Kiel asked, waiting for the other shoe to drop.

"We do not have the hauling capacity to transport more than a few hundred at most," *Ground Control* Lau replied. "We would need a dedicated troop transport, at a minimum, but those are likely to be military vessels and taking one would be difficult with our current staffing. Someone suggested we capture a cruise ship."

Lan watched a number of heads turn towards an Anglo man with dark hair who suddenly crimsoned with blush. Was this the originator of the idea?

Lan felt Kiel turn towards him with a quizzical face.

"Most ships would probably be filled with guests at any point that you approached it," she said with a frown. "Those vessels maintain fixed courses, but do not have any sort of deadhead built in, so you might be dealing with hundreds or possibly thousands of prisoners. I'm not sure that improves your logistics."

"Crap," Lau muttered under her breath.

"What was your other option please?" Kiel spoke into the rising murmurs.

"The other option involved running for home with some or all of this squadron and coming back with a large invasion force," Kosnett explained. "Assuming we can convince the fleet to spare the ships necessary."

"Have you considered a hospital ship?" Lan asked before he was even aware of himself speaking.

"A what?" Lau turned to face him.

"Hospital ship," Lan repeated. "Those fly circuits of less-developed worlds, providing more advanced medical support than smaller colonies can perhaps sustain on their own. And they are on fixed schedules."

"Dearest?" Kiel asked, concern underlying her tones.

"These men have been captured by *The Eldest* and sentenced to a lifetime of internal exile, rather than ever being sent home," Lan turned his anguish on her. "I can't imagine that the crew would resist the effort to help, if they were truly dedicated to their purpose. And many of the former prisoners would probably be in sad shape, because I cannot imagine *The Holding* provides such services."

"Are you sure?" Kosnett asked in turn.

"I cannot speak for a medical professional, Director," Lan said. "But it is the only ethical solution I can suggest. Perhaps you should return home and bring an invading horde instead?"

"If they're worth their Hippocratic Oath, I can speak for them," the blushing man suddenly leaned forward and slammed an apparently angry fist onto the tabletop hard enough to make everyone jump. "And if they aren't, then someone needs to remind them what they are all about."

Ground Control Lau turned to this man now, studying him for several seconds.

"Careful, Andre," she said in a voice that was only partly teasing. "I might have to put you in command of such a ship."

Lan watched a complex set of emotions range across the stranger's face. Anger, fear, and empathy were preeminent.

"Veitengruber," the stranger called *Andre* said to a man wearing a traditional *Aquitaine* Centurion's uniform next to *Lady Blackbeard*. Possibly for Lan and Kiel's benefit. "How were you treated?"

"I was a slave," the man replied in a cold, distant voice with traces of deep anger buried underneath and starting to bubble to the surface. "My choice was to work or starve, doing whatever tasks the overseer decided I should undertake."

"Should we kidnap a group of medical professionals and hijack their ship in order to rescue more of your comrades?" *Ground Control* continued.

"I would suggest something good for the gander, Andre," the man said. "But we're the nice guys, so keeping them as slaves of the Empire for the rest of their lives is not an ethical position. But they can settle for a few months of discomfort until Phil lets them go."

Director Kosnett turned to the blond man next to him, the temporary First Officer that Lan thought was named Evan.

"Find me the circuit," Kosnett ordered in a dark voice. "At the least, we'll take one and see if it suits our needs, or if we should just sail it home and turn it over to the Fleet before we come back to stomp on some rats."

Lan felt a chill run through his very soul at the Director's tone. He had known hard men in his time, but had never heard such a simple turn of phrase that sounded so implacably lethal.

Kosnett turned to Lan and Kiel now and bowed his head.

"Thank you," he said simply.

And just like that, the storm was gone from his face, like it had never been. But Lan would never forget those eyes. He suspected they might factor in nightmares for many years.

Lan wanted to ask why the war these people had started was accelerating, but he turned to the Centurion who claimed to have been a slave. He was a tall, almost lanky man with brown hair and a forgettable face, but there was something burning there now.

"Sri?" Lan asked.

"We have not been properly introduced, Xi Arakh Goran Lan and Nu Ulap Narah Kiel," he said in a harsh voice striving to be level and calm. "For seven years, after I was captured at *Samara*, I was a slave on *Abakn*. I worked on a cattle ranch similar to this one. I was once Imperial Flight Lieutenant Granville Veitengruber, but I have chosen to take up arms as a member of the *Republic of Aquitaine* Navy now. I will see *Mansi* liberated if it is the last thing I do."

Lan felt Kiel take his hand under the table. Up until now, Director Kosnett and his forces had been engaged in a simple war. This was larger.

This felt like Armageddon.

And he was going to help.

GROWING UP (NOVEMBER 3, 402)

Andre felt a presence more or less materialize on his right, but he didn't look away from the sun just about to slide behind the western mountains and plunge this valley into sudden darkness. It made a nice metaphor for his life, recently.

Shit was getting weird.

Rather than speak, the stranger leaned against the same fence rail, weight forward and enjoying the silence.

Andre glanced over after a time, expecting Heather. He was shocked nearly out of his senses that it was Veitengruber, the newest recruit.

The former pilot was everything Andre wasn't. Tall, blond, ruggedly handsome. Even relatively skinny compared to Andre's overall squishiness. Of course, the man had spent seven years as a slave on a cattle ranch, so doing hard work on a daily basis, rather than sitting down in medbay being fat and happy with Kermit and Max.

And apparently, the man was silent. Andre was amazed

that he just stood there, watching the cattle in the near distance and the sunset.

Did he miss being on a ranch? Doing all these things? Andre couldn't understand why he would. The man had his own command now, a warship no less, and would be able to take his revenge on the people who had imprisoned him.

Finally, Andre couldn't take the silence anymore.

"What drives you?" he asked.

It was a really good opening question for a nurse dealing with patients. You listened to their wants and needs, to their hopes and fears, knowing that such information helped you treat them better and faster, getting them back into the line.

"I would have said hatred," the man said after a pause so long Andre thought that maybe he hadn't heard the question. "But that's not who I am, or who I want to be."

Andre nodded. Those were concepts he understood He believed human were always striving to be the best version of themselves that they could manage right now. Hopefully, tomorrow will be an even better self.

"Fear, I think," Veitengruber suggested after another pause.

"Fear?" Andre asked, shocked.

This man had survived something Andre figured would have killed him long ago. And come out in a position of authority.

"I wake up some mornings and just lay there for a second before I remember where I am," Veitengruber continued. "Thinking I'm back on *Abakn* and it's time to go milk cows. That everything has just been a wild fantasy and I've never left."

"Ah," Andre said. "I understand that. All I ever wanted to do was be a nurse and help people. I only got this job because we only had three medical professionals, and Heather needed a 2IC who was an officer. Plus one who understood logistics and supply."

"What drives you?" the Imperial asked. "You seemed agitated, back there in the meeting this morning. Far more so than I would have expected, even in the little time I've known you."

"Unprofessional behavior," Andre finally realized. He had fallen silent for several seconds himself, finding the words. "The possibility that a group of doctors and nurses might not immediately come to the aid of someone, even of former enemies in need. That is not the oath we swear when we take this job."

"Does *The Holding* do it the same way, you suppose?" the lanky man asked.

"You tell me," Andre fired back. "You're the expert here."

"Before you and Doctor Hanley, the last physician I saw was the one who handled my intake, when I was first taken prisoner," Veitengruber said. "I was hosed down naked, given a battery of shots, handed a stack of new clothes, and thrown into a cell. Had I chosen to hang myself in that tiny room, I don't think they would have cared all that much."

"So how did you end up on *Abakn*?" Andre asked.

"No clue," he said simply. "The ship bounced in and out of JumpSpace for about three weeks, I think, counting by the meals served. By the time we got there, I was so starved for human contact that I went willingly when they took us to the surface. Five of us. I ended up on that ranch, with no idea what happened to the rest."

"Where's Deni from?" Andre probed carefully.

Malondenishk Abarantakratar. *Deni.*

Veitengruber's partner in ways that the Empire would never allow and the Republic wouldn't even notice. Consenting adults. You found love where you did.

Andre supposed that Phil keeping Deni on *CS-405* was a way of ensuring some level of cooperation from Veitengruber, since he wouldn't run off in his ship without his mate. Andre wasn't about to suggest that out loud.

"*NovLao* is more or less on the far side of *The Holding,*" the man said, eyes distant. "They're smaller than the Empire, maybe the size of the Republic, more or less, but not as integrated or as technologically advanced. *Buran* has been pushing them back for generations, consuming one planet after another."

"Where will you two call home?"

Andre had only gotten snippets of the story, up until now.

"*Aquitaine,* for now," the man replied. "Nobody knows what shape *NovLao* is in. He's been gone for more than five years, and hasn't seen any of his own countrymen in that time. *Buran* might have won."

Andre nodded. It would be hell to be without a country, but at least they had a place to hide, while they sorted it out.

The silence stretched out for a companionable space.

"I'm also afraid of letting Admiral Kosnett down," the Imperial admitted out of the blue. "And Heather."

Andre nodded in sympathy. It was a fear he woke with regularly, as well. That the hard-core professionals would need something from him and he wouldn't be able to deliver it. That people might die because he wasn't up to some task they had trusted him with.

"Knowing those two, they're more afraid of getting everyone killed for no reason," Andre offered. "With nothing to show for it."

"It's war," Veitengruber replied. "People die."

"Yeah, but Phil could have gone home already and been considered successful," Andre said. "Every day we're at this, there's a risk someone stumbles upon us, or a ship breaks down again, and they lose people."

"So we should head home?" the ex-pilot turned his head to stare.

"I'm surprised that Phil didn't load you up with food and a crew and send you for help already, man," Andre smiled grimly. "Not a lot that little boat can do against most things, but you sure as hell could get a message to the right people faster than we could."

"*Persephone* might surprise you, Andre," Veitengruber said.

"No," Andre countered. "That ship? Not at all. You? You already have. And continue to. People like you mean we'll win this war."

The Imperial fell silent at that. Andre felt his face turn back to the sun, just finally vanishing beneath the crest. The light vanished with the heat.

After another minute or two of silence, the man took his weight off the rail, stretched his back, and turned.

"Thank you," Veitengruber said, turning the rest of the way and walking back to the main house.

Andre considered the breeze that was starting to turn chilly. They all lived with fear of failure. Veitengruber was just perhaps closer to it, having been trapped for so long. But he was also a good example of walking forward each day until he escaped.

Fake it until you make it.

That was something Andre figured he could do, too.

PLANNING THE RAID (NOVEMBER 4, 402)

"Okay, what evil have you two come up with?" a voice intruded.

Siobhan looked up and grinned at Heather. Felt Trinidad do the same.

The bridge of *Queen Anne's Revenge* was cozy with three people, but Siobhan had wanted to have this conversation away from everyone else. Especially with all the noise outside. And all the racket starting up downstairs.

She closed the hatch once Heather was clear of the tracks and spun sideways in the captain's seat. She gestured *Ground Control* to sit as well, in one of the two jumpseats on the side walls especially for passengers.

"So we don't know if they'll start escorting hospital ships around," Siobhan began with a small laugh. "They haven't in the past, but there are all these dangerous pirates running around right now, and *Buran*'s had enough time to maybe shift some extra Hammerheads into the sector. Anything with guns chases us off at this point."

"And Phil and Evan will scout this one pretty hard before committing," Heather completed the thought. "So either we scrub and run home at that point, or catch them with their pants down."

"Yup, so I figure they've got one of two options when *Persephone* suddenly drops out of Jump and orders them to heave to," Siobhan said.

"Why Granville?" Heather probed.

"Option One: the Director over there suddenly has a gunship on his flank and rolls over politely rather than fleeing or fighting," Siobhan continued. "We're been hitting various places, but just robbing people, and not committing mass casualties. Maybe they figure they can negotiate with us, or they're buying time to jailbreak later."

"Gotcha," *Ground Control* said. "Option Two?"

"The Director panics and triggers a blind jump, figuring he can get away from a single Imperial cutter trapped inside the gravity well," Siobhan answered. "Goes random, but not that far."

"Except they don't do random," Heather said. "They'll have a Jump planned and programmed into the system, specifically to escape pirates."

"Yup, and that's where I come in," *Stunt Dude* entered the fray. "*Buran*'s predictable. Where's the first place he'd jump in a hurry?"

"Straight up, about 20 AU," Heather smiled suddenly. "Like an armadillo."

"*Si, Jefe*," Trinidad grinned. "So what happens when

he does that and Phil's sitting right there with *405* and a whole bunch of guns?"

"You board him, either invited in or just like we did to take *Packmule*," Heather grinned back.

"Yup," *Stunt Dude* said.

"So what if he doesn't?" Heather turned to Siobhan.

Lady Blackbeard nodded. That was where it got tricky.

"Maybe he escapes us," she replied. "Maybe he flees the system and goes to get help. We'll be long gone before they get back, but the locals will be all wound up anyway."

"Okay," Heather's face turned serious. "In the *RAN*, hospital ships are military. In *Buran*, that would mean *Sentient*, even with a human crew. What do we do then?"

"As far as I know, the Hammerhead is the smallest *Sentient* ship's hull," Siobhan said. "If he's not one of those, then my guess is a largely civilian vessel. But that is exactly the risk we take doing this. Everybody's keen to make one last big splash, because every bit of wildfire we can set makes it that much easier for Jessica and the Grand Admiral, when they start the next campaign. The old fart's got to be considering pulling some of his warships off the border to handle internal security duties, which just makes it that much harder to hold anyplace except *Samara*. We're punching way above our weight here."

"So you find a hospital ship," Heather said to Trinidad. "Then what? Or rather, how?"

"Everyone who can hold a stunner and fit in a suit goes over," he said in a much more serious tone. "*Packmule* had almost no crew, and we hit them blind in deep space. This ship's likely to have hundreds of crew, maybe thousands, but most of them are just going to be medical techs, and not sailors or marines. Hell, I'd have had most of my marines down on the surface protecting any teams I had on the ground. So maybe we can control those we have left."

"Do we dump most of the crew on the planet?" Heather asked both of them. "Load them onto a lander and be done with them?"

"Dunno," Siobhan felt her shoulders crawl up into a shrug. "Too many maybes and what-abouts to plan concretely. I want the hull and the facilities. Maybe we ask for volunteers and watch them like hawks?"

"And we won't know anything until we're already in control of *Mansi* and needing the ship itself," Heather continued the thought. "I'm still teetering on scrubbing the whole operation and bringing in Jessica."

"Let's at least see what they've got, Heather," Siobhan turned serious. "Panic over there is almost as good as us pulling a jailbreak, going back to Phil's original plans. And those guys on *Mansi* aren't going anywhere if it takes us another year."

"Okay," Heather replied nervously. "How's the build-out downstairs coming?"

"Slowly, but Markus has confidence they can pull it off, after they fix *Persephone*," Siobhan perked up. "Turns out the entire mechanism is smaller than the truck we normally carry, but not by much, so we are going to remove the front ramp for now and build a solid bow with a slot where the beam emitter itself will stick through."

"Can we undo it later?" Heather asked. "Phil's planning on giving this ship up."

"Have you asked Kiel if she wants an armed freighter?" Trinidad laughed.

That was good for a couple of giggles. Commercial, private freighters weren't armed in *Buran*. Ever. The only ships with guns also had *Sentient* Systems controlling them, so that the God in charge of *The Holding* had complete authority.

"Seriously, though," Trinidad continued. "I figure we'll end up buying them a new one. This hull is going to be too well known and eventually someone throws them in prison as accessories, just for having it, regardless of the truth."

"Makes sense," Heather said. She stood. "Let me know what you need when we have the cutter finished. Figure that's going to take about a week, with the crew we've got grinding and polishing over there."

"Will do, boss," Siobhan said, triggering the hatch and watching the woman depart.

Heather had the heaviest load. Phil was in command, but he had to stay aboard *CS-405* as much as possible, so Heather was in charge out in the field.

Ground Control.

And it was only going to get worse.

MORE NEW RECRUITS (NOVEMBER 4, 402)

THEY WERE all up on the bridge of *Persephone*, sitting or standing as they could in the cramped space that was designed for three to be working and only a couple of others standing in corners.

Granville was standing in the space immediately behind the captain's chair. His captain's chair. Except he would be flying the vessel himself, rather than supervising a bridge crew of two.

The five in front of him were the absolute minimum a vessel like this required in order to be in combat, and even that was stretching the definition. He had lost Galin, back to his regular duty aboard *Packmule*, although the man was aft right now, working on the engines.

Isiah had remained, the farm boy from the outskirts of Penmerth on *Ladaux*, where his parents were apparently vaguely distant neighbors of the famous Jessica Keller he had heard bits and pieces about from the rest of the team. Isiah was a quiet kid. Skinny, with an auburn cowlick that went crazy if he didn't keep his hair buzzed tight on top. He was still in charge of life support and control systems, basically anything that wasn't one of the engines or generators. He was probably in over his head, but they all were. And he was busting his ass every day.

First-Rate-Spacer Arla Bardeen had taken over for Galin back in the engine room, expected to do the job of five people, like the rest of them. She was as opposite as possible from Isiah: a Chinese Diaspora city girl from *Anameleck Prime*, one of the most industrial planets in the galaxy, as he understood it.

As close to a First Officer as Granville was going to get was Vicente Leomiti, one of *CS-405*'s Gunner's Mates who had just been promoted to Yeoman and Gunner for this duty. At twenty-six years standard, the short, swarthy man was the second oldest crewman, behind Granville. He was, according to what others had said, trying to fill the role the former Boatswain, Bok Battenhouse the cowboy, had been doing on *CS-405*, by being the grand old veteran.

He was doing an acceptable job for now, growing into being responsible for everyone. And he would be too busy, much of the time, since he was responsible for laying and supervising the Type-3 beam in the bow. And doing it without four aides.

First-Rate-Spacer Minh Morgan, the starboard Type-1 gunner, was quiet, shy, and competent. His ancestry looked mostly Anglo, with some Chinese Diaspora thrown in, but after ten thousand years, were there any left with a single culture for ancestors? He didn't talk much, but got the job done. Granville was fine with that. Eventually, he would either come out of his shell or they would be home and this crew probably broken up and returned to their old duties.

The last crew member was the most interesting, at least to Granville's sensibilities. Able-Spacer Sharri Spier had been a Landsman until this week, the *Aquitaine* equivalent of a simple Trooper in the Imperial Fleet, and not even a Petty Officer of some sort, like the others. Just a child, even though she was nineteen standard. The others had somewhere between three and, in his case, twelve years' experience on her.

This had been her first duty assignment out of advanced training. *CS-405* was the first ship she had ever served on, and she had joined not long before the great raid that caused *CS-405* to become forlorn. And for her second duty, she was his port Type-1 Gunner.

Physically, it was still a shock to see her, even though he had one other female in his new crew. Spier was of a softer version of the African Diaspora she referred to as Carrib, so her distant ancestors had come to the so-called New Worlds of America as slaves, and then bred with their masters and the local inhabitants to produce a new ethnotype.

Her skin was darker than his, but not as dark as traditional African Diaspora. Weathered oak rather than charcoal or chocolate, perhaps mixed with a hint of gold underneath to give it luster and value.

Granville wasn't particularly interested in girls, but she was a striking woman, even as young as she was. Nervous as hell right now, but holding her shoulders back and eyeing him levelly as if she would fight him for her right to stand on his deck.

Yes, she would do.

Granville took a deep breath and let it go. This would be easier to face if he had Deni here with him, but he had no doubt of the man's love, and that would carry him over almost any obstacle.

"I've never been one for speeches," he said simply. "And I've spent the last seven years being a slave on a cattle ranch, so I'm out of the habit of command. You will need to remind me occasionally that I'm in charge, because I might forget."

That broke the ice with them for an embarrassed chuckle.

He was a stranger, while they had all at least served together aboard *CS-405*, part of a crew of just over two hundred that had relied on one another in the worst circumstances.

"But we are a warship in Her Majesty's service," he continued. "I understand that some of your officers have actually met Karl VIII, back when she was Centurion *Wiegand*. I look forward to taking you all to her Court, as I was once an Imperial officer, and this, an Imperial vessel. *Persephone* represented the Seventeenth Imperial Police Protectorate at one time, so we have their proud standards to live up to, as well as the *Republic of Aquitaine* Navy's. And we will."

He paused long enough to scan their faces again, to make sure they understood the seriousness of his purpose.

"Admiral Kosnett will have us at the sharpest point of conflict," Granville intoned. "*Packmule* and *Queen Anne's*

Revenge are not armed, and cannot fight, even after the spare turret is mounted in the freighter. *CS-405* is too valuable to risk. That leaves us to go where the risk is greatest and the guns the hottest. I was once a fighter pilot, in the era before, and that was our task then, as well. Normally, this vessel would have a crew of nearly forty. The six of us are all that Admiral Kosnett and *Ground Control* can spare. Questions?"

"Can we do it, sir?" Spier asked after raising her hand and him nodding.

"Or die trying, Spier," Granville replied.

"Can we really pull off a jailbreak?" Isiah raised his voice.

"If it comes to that point, I expect there is a reasonable chance that this ship is destroyed in the attempt," Granville let the seriousness of the situation fill his voice.

The others flinched, but only a little. They were sailors, and volunteers for this duty.

"The plan I have seen calls for us to come out of Jump at the highest possible speed, aimed at one of the stations," he continued. "We would fire as many missiles as the engineers can mount on the outside of the hull and hope that they eliminate the station as a threat before they can hit us with something like a Type-4 beam. Unlike cruisers, something that heavy would simply cut us in half, sending the flaming fragments into the atmosphere where our only hope would be to hit the lifepods and add ourselves to the list of prisoners and slaves on the planet below. It is a risk worth taking."

Nods. Volunteers. Warriors, even the babe in the

woods with this crew, Spier, who would be responsible for keeping incoming missiles off their flank.

"Anything else?" he asked after a long silence.

It was much to absorb.

"Then I will return you to your duties," Granville said. "I expect us to take our first training flight in four days, running out to find something we can use to calibrate the guns on. Until then, you are responsible for overseeing the crews assigned to repair and tune your stations, regardless of the rank of the others involved."

He turned his attention to Spier, specifically.

"That means you give Yeoman Galin Tuason orders when he's working on your gun, Able-Spacer," Granville made it plain. "Understood?"

The nod he got back was a bit rabbity, but it would have to do.

They were all going to have to grow into their jobs, even a breveted command centurion who hadn't been in combat in seven years.

THE POSSE (NOVEMBER 5, 402)

THE WORST PART of it all was how much fun Trinidad was having, walking forty-one candidates for marine firearms training through their paces on a gun range that had been cleared of cows and set up with targets. The morning was gloriously sunny, with only the slightest breeze out of the east. Four lines had been established, with targets, lanes, and tables; for people to practice gun safety, accuracy, and preparation. It was time to rock.

Acting had been fun. Being a stuntman had been even better.

But being a teacher had lit a small fire under his ass. Gave him an utter runner's high when somebody finally got it and suddenly turned into Six-Gun Sally on his range.

Phil, Heather, and Siobhan had no idea what they would be facing when they went for what he kept thinking of as Act Three of the Great Action Adventure Tentpole Summer Movie.

Our heroes have escaped almost-certain death or capture, fleeing into the wilderness one step ahead of The Law. They've had little adventures in the swamp, building up their strength and willpower, but it was finally time to emerge and challenge the evil overlord for control of the galaxy.

Or something like that.

Maybe he'd take up screenwriting when he retired from active duty. Add that to everything else and open his own school to train actors, stuntbabes, and writers how to make big and impressive movies with physical stunts, rather than doing it all on a green screen and a computer.

Wind in your hair, and explosions behind you, while you're flying through the air and one of your marines is getting it all on his helmet cam.

'Cause we can. And we have.

And now, it was almost time. Nearly a quarter of the overall crew would be tasked with possibly boarding an enemy vessel and taking it under fire. Most of them were ready.

Nakisha was having a brief and apparently rumbly discussion with someone down on the end. She turned to him with a silent plea for help, so Trinidad put on his *Stunt Dude* persona and stomped over.

"Problems?" he asked, feeling like the sheriff strutting into the bar in a western.

"Why do I have to do this?" Andre Gave almost snarled at him, willing to take his anger out on another officer, but not the sailor just trying to teach him. "I took the Hippocratic Oath to do no harm, damn it."

"It's a stunner, Andre," Trinidad pointed out in a dry voice. "The worst you can hurt someone is they fall over and bash their head on the ground accidentally. There will only be five of us with lethal weapons when we do this. And Nakisha here is the only one playing with high explosives."

"I'm a nurse, man," Andre's voice turned to pleading.

"No, sir," Nakisha's humor finally snapped, apparently. "You are an officer who is expected to take command of the vessel when we capture it for you. Act like one, damn it."

For the briefest moment, Trinidad wondered if Andre was going to punch her. He might have, in that situation. And nobody would press charges.

Back home, them qualified as fighting words.

After a moment, Andre's eyes grew shrouded and still. Finally, he blew out a heavy breath. Muttered something ugly under his breath that everyone pretended not to hear.

The man turned back to the downrange portion of things and stepped up to the little table that held the stunner pistol. He lifted it left handed, muttering all the while, and pointed it at the sky, just like he had been taught, finger off the trigger and weapon next to his ear, where the only threat was to stupid birds.

"Only way I can certify you for a boarding action, Andre," Trinidad said just loud enough to cover the profanities leaking out of the man like a failing dike. "And you'll have to be armed at all times while aboard a captured vessel that still has any of its crew."

More profanities. At least these were aimed at him now, and not at Nakisha. Not that she was a fragile blossom, but Trinidad didn't hold grudges like that woman could.

She looked at him with a silent question. He nodded and she stepped back from being rangemaster, leaving the task to him. Trinidad stepped into the spot and came to stillness, hoping a little of it would rub off on Andre.

The first shot was low and a little to the right. Normal. Someone expecting recoil like a pulse pistol or a slugthrower had. And jerking the trigger rather than caressing it. You had to be gentle on a trigger like that. Always with a smooth motion until you got the results you wanted.

Who knew that learning guns would make him better in bed?

"Gently," Trinidad offered. "It won't bite. You will."

Andre nodded unconsciously and blew out a breath, like Nakisha had been trying to teach him. Second shot was still low, but not as bad. Pulling with some flinch, but he could work with that.

"Trigger's softer than that, Andre," he said. "Just caress it and let it do all the work."

Behind him, Nakisha snickered. Probably blushing, but he wasn't going to look. All marines told the same dirty jokes on the gun range to new recruits.

Better.

Third shot had gotten high enough to count on the target signaler. Still right, but Trinidad was used to that.

"Shift your feet a little, Andre," he ordered politely. "Move your right foot forward twenty centimeters."

"Why?"

"You'll see."

He did and aimed again. Fourth shot set all the flashing lights off on the target dummy.

"What happened?" Andre asked as he waited for it to reset.

"Natural cross-over on your hands," Trinidad said. "Normally, I would have you keep shooting square until your hands adjusted. Easier right now to just get you in the habit of turning a little when you need to shoot."

"Huh," he muttered. "Now what?"

"Now we walk you through the whole process slowly," Trinidad said. "From full extension down to quick-draw. Once you have that, you get your little boarding action crew card and we can go play cowboy."

"It's a hospital ship, Trinidad," Andre countered in a voice reaching for angry again.

"No, it isn't," *Stunt Dude* said. "It is an enemy warship, crewed by people that might try to kill you. You have to be ready to stop them, if they decide to take the ship back."

"By killing people?" Angry Andre was back. His head turned, but the gun never wavered from the target.

"No," Trinidad growled. "That's my job. You have to be in command over there, so they'll listen to you and not try something stupid. Otherwise, Nakisha and I might have to kill people. That's what this is trying to prevent."

"Stupid idea," Andre muttered under his breath.

"Welcome to the Navy, Marine," Trinidad fired back.

GRANVILLE STUDIED *Persephone* by the light of the sun just coming over the eastern peaks. He was probably never going to manage to sleep as late as dawn again in his life, so he was up early to do things. It didn't help that he was sleeping alone, so he didn't even had Deni to snuggle up against for warmth.

They had built a crane. And a dock big enough for both *Anna* and *Persephone*. The latter was inside there now, getting the last bits of work done, which involved dropping back in a blower system that had frozen from grit hidden inside. Easier to pull and repack the bearings on the ground, especially when you could pop open outer panels and just lift the whole mechanism.

Footsteps behind him caused Granville to glance back. This early, only the folks with cattle and chicken duties were up, plus the kitchen staff. Nobody was over here.

Able-Spacer Spier walked close, holding something flat in her hands.

"Here, sir," she said, handing him something. "I had these made up for everyone."

"What is it?" he asked, turning the cloth object over in his hands.

"Fleet patches, sir," she smiled up at him. "Seventeenth Imperial Police Protectorate. Found it in the computers when I asked someone to dig. Figured we needed something special for *Persephone*, but I'm not an artist. Maybe we commission someone to create us a ship's patch, too?"

It was shaped like a kiteshield patch, a little larger than his palm. Stylized image of a police cutter with two stars in the background, with the writing all the way around the top and sides.

The pirates aboard *Queen Anne's Revenge* wore civilian clothing. Claimed it got them into character, which made sense, as they were all characters in some bizarre vid. *Ground Control's* crew on *Packmule* wore *RAN* uniforms, including Deni, who had been temporarily inducted, with the understanding he could resign when they got someplace safe.

Granville and his people wore the same black-and-green of the *RAN*, with *CS-405* on their left shoulder.

Fleet Patch was an Imperial thing. It went on the right shoulder with a temporary burr-and-hook backing to show where a ship belonged. The last ship's patch he had worn before *CS-405* had been *IFV Germania*. The last fleet patch was Fourteenth Fleet, stationed out of *Osynth B'Udan*.

"Why?" Granville asked after studying it for a moment, completely at a loss.

"The others are civilians, sir," Spier replied with conviction. "But we're an Imperial warship, even if most of us came from *Aquitaine* originally. And like you said, we need to represent the Seventeenth as well. What better way to do that, especially when we get home and they make us heroes?"

He fixed her with a firm eye, a commanding officer taking the measure of a new sailor, but the woman was almost transparent both in her confidence and her innocent naivety. She truly believed that this was the right thing to do. And she was far closer to all the training and patriotism of service than he was.

It had been so long that he had forgotten what that was like. And he had no idea if it was appropriate, from either an Imperial or Republic standpoint, if the lawyers wanted to get involved.

But it felt right.

He held it up to the point of his shoulder, trying to get a feel for how it would sit. Imperial uniforms were much looser in fit, unlike the tunic he wore right now, stretched over his shoulders.

"Let me, sir?" she asked, moving around to the side.

One hand carefully peeled the backing, and then she grabbed his far side and held him steady while she stuck it on. He would have to add some tack stitches later, to hold the patch in place, but it would stay with him for a few days of movement, at a minimum.

He craned his head around and held up his arm to see the effect.

"Is good?" she asked nervously, maybe suddenly aware

that an Able-Spacer wasn't supposed to take this much initiative.

"It's perfect," he replied, thinking about it. "Do you have a second one handy?"

"Yes, sir."

She pulled it from a pocket inside her tunic and handed it over.

Granville studied the thing for a second before he figured out how to get the backing off.

"Your turn," he said, moving around her so he could attach the patch to the woman in turn.

He liked the way her face lit up when she saw it on her shoulder. Professional pride.

He hadn't felt something like that in years. That sense of belonging to something greater was why he had joined in the first place.

"You have more?" he asked quietly.

She nodded, biting her lips nervously.

"Good," he said. "Let's go roust the rest and get them properly uniformed this morning for breakfast."

"I done good?" Spier asked.

For a moment, Granville blanked, but then he remembered that she was barely nineteen years old, possibly less than two years removed from high school.

"You did excellent, Spier," he reassured her. "After this, we'll get this design painted on the outside of the hull, on the left side of the forward airlock hatch. Then we'll find us an artist to do a ship's patch for *Persephone* and have more patches and standards made."

"Thank you, sir."

She fell in next to him as he turned and headed back

to the main house. He had a smile on his face this morning. He couldn't remember the last time that had happened. Usually neutral reserve, or scowls. But not joy.

But yes, *Persephone* needed a logo. She was a warship. She was in service, protecting the Empire.

And so was he.

TASK FORCE (DECEMBER 3, 402)

SIOBHAN LOOKED at the display on her tiny bridge as *Persephone* completed her climb to orbit and joined them. As usual, *Stunt Dude* was in the right-hand seat. Everyone else was in back somewhere, doing stuff.

The front quarter of the cargo deck below her had been sealed off with a bulkhead, and the front ramp removed and replaced with a solid bow. First-Rate-Spacer Harriette Neitz had joined the crew as gunner to handle the narwhal horn that had been installed, so she was probably checking that, with Markus in her side pocket with all his tools, just in case.

They had made training runs, alone and with *Persephone*, blowing up asteroids and stuff, but this was the real thing. Time to go hunting.

Queen Anne would be the forward scout, as always. *CS-405* would sneak along the fringes. *Packmule* would stay well behind the front and keep everybody fed. And

Granville Veitengruber would be pushing the envelope in his own way.

Siobhan smiled at the thought.

He had the only properly working primary JumpSail system. *CS-405* was still running on her repaired backup, and the spare one on *Persephone* had simply been too small and the wrong everything to cut it out and install it on an *RAN* vessel. The two freighters used old-fashioned *Buran* JumpDrives.

So Granville could range faster and farther than anyone else, since he didn't need to drop out of JumpSpace regularly and throw himself across multi-space. Plus he had guns. If they hadn't needed *Anna* to be able to fly right up to someone all innocent-like, she might have recommended letting Lan and Kiel go and piling all her pirates in with Veitengruber.

But she could still sneak in places none of the others could. And she had a gun now, too. Big one. No defensive artillery, so she had to steer clear of combat, but nobody would be expecting a teeny, little freighter likes hers to have a bite. It would be like facing a carnivorous rabbit or something.

"What's so funny?" *Stunt Dude* asked from the side seat.

Whoops. Giggle with the inside voice next time.

"First time we actually shoot at someone," *Lady Blackbeard* replied with a charming laugh. "Won't they be surprised."

"Oh, yeah."

A console light came on, indicating communications.

"*Queen Anne's Revenge*," she replied, waiting for everyone to check in.

"All hands, this is Acting Fleet Centurion Kosnett," Phil announced.

She and Heather had finally gotten him to admit that they were a full task force now, and not just a garage band. He needed to pretend to be the boss, and not just the commanding officer of the largest ship. The Imperials would have classified him as a Commodore at Captain's rank, but Phil was *RAN* to his bones.

"*Task Force Barnaul* is now operational," he continued, naming them for that first raid where *Anna* had gone on the offensive.

Resolute Revolution didn't count, because that was almost accidental, and they were giving the ship back later. Maybe. Or something.

Privately, the betting was that *Anna* would be properly impressed into service and Kiel and Lan paid cash for the hull, with the understanding that they would turn around and buy a freighter from the Imperials. And the assembled crew of *CS-405* would all chip in to buy them a full cargo before they went home.

"We will maintain formation as much as possible until we congregate at Layover Delta," Phil ordered the ships, knowing that nobody was going to make anything like the same speed across.

Persephone could fly straight there in one shot. *CS-405* could do something similar, but still needed to drop out to cool things off and realign the matrix regularly. *Anna* would be almost as fast as *405*, and *Packmule* would lumber along in their wake.

"At that point, we will begin scouting our target for the assault," Phil's voice had grown even harder and more serious than normal now. "I will remind you, unnecessarily, that stealth is critical, if we wish the second part of this campaign to succeed, so everyone will continue to maintain the highest standards of conduct for the *RAN*. And the Seventeenth Imperial Police Protectorate."

Siobhan pictured Veitengruber turning beet red at those words, even as his crew cheered. They had updated their uniforms to reflect *Persephone*'s temporary ensign, at least until they could get back to civilization and have *Aquitaine*'s First Lord give it her blessing. And maybe Fourth Lord. Assuming the Emperor didn't just overrule them.

The woman just might.

Veitengruber had been an Imperial officer first. And that had been an Imperial hull. And Seventeenth Imperial Police Protectorate would have a strong opinion, as well.

Better make them all look good.

"*Queen Anne's Revenge*, you have the flag," Phil ordered.

"All hands, this is Siobhan Skokomish, aboard *Queen Anne's Revenge*. I have the flag," she said calmly, letting the lasers send her words across the entire Task Force. "All vessels, conform to my heading and prepare for JumpSpace."

She looked over at *Stunt Dude*. He was practically vibrating with excitement, like a dog on a car ride, or a kid that needed to pee. But this would be his show, if they launched an assault.

She reached out a hand and selected the menu for the JumpDrives on her screen.

The big, purple button flashed once, indicating a full charge on the system and everything ready to go.

Queen Anne's Revenge leapt out of the universe.

WEASELS IN THE HEN HOUSE
(JANUARY 3, 403)

EVERY SOLAR SYSTEM WAS QUIET, when you were sitting clear out on the south-pole-inner-fringe of the Oort Cloud. Phil enjoyed the view from here as *CS-405* pretended to be another comet drifting in the darkness.

Kyzyl was a fairly new colony, according to Kiel's notes on the sector. Another one that had been established just before the war with the *Fribourg Empire* suddenly turned hot enough to choke off resources in the interior. In forty years, they had built a single town on a nice harbor, with farmers slowly working their way inland up the two main rivers, and a series of fishing communities up and down the coast in both directions.

Total planetary population today was around fifteen million, with pitifully-few exports of note. Kiel and her husband had never been here, because it was well off the main trade routes, and the people on the planet were probably at least another generation from making enough above survival to make it profitable to even come here.

That was one of the reasons that the DeathGod in charge sent hospital ships to various outposts on a semi-regular circuit. According to the notes, the only hospital on the planet had maybe fifty beds, total, and the only medical staff had been sent here from somewhere else.

Poor, backwards, and isolated. Prime targets for pirates.

Phil didn't enjoy this part of his job, even knowing they were the enemy. People would die because of him. And not in war, where it was an acceptable outcome. Children wouldn't get some life-saving surgery if he was successful, because the doctors never came.

He was a farmer culling sheep for the winter, deciding who would live and who would not. War was hell, and in some ways he was no better than *Buran*.

Until he remembered a prison planet a long ways away from here. Filled with men who wouldn't even get something like a hospital ship to fix simple problems. They would just die from basic things.

Fribourg and *Aquitaine* had been at war off and on for several centuries, but prisoners taken in combat were always traded home in fairly short order. Perhaps a year in a transfer camp at most, and then you were back with your loved ones, or back on duty.

These men were the forgotten. The Lost.

Phil would see them home. The only question was how much damage he had to do to *The Holding* first.

"Evan," he finally stirred from the hypnotic images on his screen. "What's the latest?"

"Assuming they're not using some complicated misdirection code, they'll be breaking orbit in roughly ninety hours, sir," the Science Officer replied quickly. "They've got a ship on the ground that's almost as big as *Cayenne*, sir. *Auberon*'s old Nightshade-class DropShip. It's a flying hospital, with full surgical capabilities and around two hundred medical personnel. That will be lifting in about a day and a half, and then docking with the main ship, prior to departure."

"And still no orbital defenses?" Phil asked.

"Negative, sir," Evan nodded. "The usual four satellites: three to mark your grid, and the fourth filled with metals and water."

"What's the squadron's supply situation?" Phil asked.

Evan was acting as First Officer, with Heather and Siobhan both gone. He needed to remember to transcend the Sciences duties and cover everyone. Especially with a task force.

Evan paused to flip through some screens on his console.

"We used a lot of metal building that dry-dock, back at the *Lighthouse*, sir," he finally replied. "We're not currently critical, but restocking would probably be a good idea, depending on our next phases."

"Make a note to let Trinidad Mildon and Markus Dunklin know," Phil decided. "If we can capture the ship cleanly enough, they can run down and fill their holds with materials from the truck stop. But have them check with me first."

"Roger that, sir," Evan said.

"I think I've seen enough, Evan," Phil said a moment later. "You?"

"Anytime, sir," he said. "Got everything I need."

"West," Phil turned to the Yeoman flying today. "Prepare to drop us into JumpSpace and take us back to everyone else."

It was time to take the war up a notch.

THE STALK (JANUARY 4, 403)

THE COMMANDERS HAD BEEN aboard *CS-405* for the final mission parameters, but Granville was home now. Back aboard *Persephone* and planning his approach.

He hadn't been in combat in nearly eight years, and for once he was happy not to share his bridge with anyone. Nobody could see how bad his hands were wanting to shake. Deni would make a joke about now that would break through all the tension.

He missed his other half. This mission had to succeed, so that they could go find their own happiness.

Everyone was at their stations, instead: Leomiti forward with Morgan and Spier on the flanks; Olshefski midship and Bardeen aft.

Persephone's bridge had been designed for three. A command officer and two specialists handling things. Given the size of the vessel, maybe only a Lieutenant, like he had been, but possibly a Lt. Commander. With maybe one or two other officers aboard at most, serving as a Chief Engineer and a Navigator.

But he was alone. As he had always been in his fightercraft. His, the sole responsibility to fly, navigate, and maintain the shields, if combat broke out. He was his own science officer as well, handling all the communication chores with everything slaved to the commander's console.

And he was about to attack, a guppy threatening a whale, except that this little fishy could bite. Granville wondered if they would actually use the guns today, or just threaten the big hospital ship, and then help the others chase it down when it decided to run.

"All hands, sixty seconds to action," he said into the intercom.

Because he couldn't see anybody right now, Granville had decided to leave the line open ship-wide, so everyone had a friendly voice somewhere close. Otherwise, they were all alone in whatever chamber their duty station required.

He had spent enough time alone on *Abakn*. At least until Deni saved his sanity.

"Engineering, confirm all systems on-line and putting out full power," he continued.

"Everything on the beam, sir," Bardeen replied with a smile in her voice. "Shield generators on and ready."

"Systems, how's life support holding?" Granville called to Isiah, his longest-serving crewmember, by only several weeks, but still a plank-holder, along with him and Galin.

"I wanna convert one of the storage lockers to a green house, sir," the man said. "Systems are still kicking up old dirt and grime and it gets a little stinky back here."

"Remind me later," Granville said. "Bow Gun?"

"We are fully charged and ready for battle, sir," Leomiti sounded like a young WarGod preparing for the end of the universe.

"Starboard Gun?" Granville continued.

"All set, sir," Morgan said quietly. He was always quiet.

"Port Gun?" Granville completed the circuit.

"Cleared and prepared for action, bridge," Spier replied crisply.

She had never seen combat, but you couldn't have told that from her voice.

Granville looked down and confirmed his own boards. He could have read the status from here, but it was better to talk to people.

He had once spent nearly a year in silence, learning Mongolian well enough to actually talk to people. Silence wore on the soul in ways that pain, physical pain, never could.

He had survived, he reminded himself. He would continue to. He had a place. He had a purpose.

And he had friends. And his love.

Now he needed to go be a hero.

"Ten seconds, everyone on your toes," Granville ordered, hearing his own voice change.

He sounded like a commander now, and not the punk-kid pilot who knew everything in the universe, right up until the moment he didn't.

Persephone emerged from the shadow of Hades and cast spring about her. He was coming in fast, but not so hot that he would blow by his target. And not close enough to the edge of the gravity well that he collapsed his matrix and had to rebuild it.

No, today he was a messenger speeding to the king with critical news from a distant battle. Nobody should panic.

At least, not yet.

Granville read the system plot on the right-hand side of his screen, while listening to the comm and keeping the left-hand side dedicated to internal gauges.

They were coming in from behind the target as it orbited. The other ship was about twenty degrees south from the planet's equator, but Granville had aimed to insert right at the ecliptic. It would look less threatening, and hopefully put him in a position to pounce if the captain over there wasn't paying attention.

He purposefully didn't hail the only other vessel in orbit, and all of his transponders read like he was a light freighter from *Ninagirsu*. Anything to put the other guy off guard, as there was nobody likely to accidentally fire on them right now.

"We are inserting into system orbit," Granville said out loud, keeping up his story-telling narration of events.

Persephone's scanners were too good and too powerful for a simple freighter, and he wasn't skilled enough to dial them down now, and then bring them back up later when he needed them, so he went in on passives instead.

CS-405 had spent two days watching, and nothing had apparently changed from the notes Evan Brinich had provided.

Slowly, Granville converged, maintaining a line twenty

degrees north of the hospital ship, but at a close elevation and closing speed.

Finally, somebody woke up. Obviously a civilian vessel, as anybody with a military background would have said something as soon as hit an orbital path.

"*DYWXK-345029*, this is *PWMGT-6357181*," a man's voice challenged over the radio. He sounded bored. "We're on an operational deployment with a designated clearance zone. You need to move to a different orbital location, or land on the planet below. Everything within thirty degrees of sky-arc is off-limits."

"Uhm, could you repeat that, please?" Granville said, putting the internals on mute so his crew could listen, but not be heard. "What's up with so much sky?"

"We're a medical vessel, *DYWXK-345029*," the man continued. "We have just retrieved our lander from the ground and will be departing soon, but you need to keep your distance. If you are landing, you should start your spiral now."

"Oh," Granville continued to play dumb. "Like, a real hospital? In space and everything?"

"You got it, buddy," the man replied. "Serving *The Holding* by taking care of outer colonies."

"So if I hadn't seen a doctor in a year…?"

"Make an appointment at our next landfall, just like everybody else. We're on a tight timeline and everything's already packed up for transit."

"Okay, good to know." Granville tried to sound relieved, disappointed, and full of wonder, all at the same time. "Gimme an hour to plot my landing, we weren't expecting anyone here, so I only had us to orbit while I got out the slide-rule and did the rest."

"Acknowledged, *DYWXK-345029*," the man said, still bored and distant. "But keep on your current heading so you don't cross our flight path."

"Gotcha," Granville said, cutting the circuit.

He reopened the intercom so everyone could hear.

"All hands, stand by while we give them time to relax," Granville smiled into the microphone.

They were coming up on the hospital ship slowly right now. Casually, as it were. And well clear, despite the other guy's insistence on thirty degrees of clearance in every direction.

It wasn't like there were any other vessels in orbit besides the two of them, so the man was just being a punk. Or a didact, which was even worse.

Granville hated barracks-lawyers.

Ship like that had next to zero acceleration, so he wasn't worried about them suddenly putting the engines into overdrive and escaping a police cutter that had just come out of the maintenance yard.

And they should be completely unarmed, except for the deadly, razor-sharp wit of the man currently being a pain in the ass on the radio.

Their only escape from big, bad pirates was going to be triggering the JumpDrives from inside the gravity well, and hoping for the best.

Pity, that.

There were two ways to do this. First, he could just kind of ooze over, playing stupid until the other guy noticed and said something. But that ran the risk of them getting away from him, and Granville really wanted this one for himself, if that was possible.

Or, he could turn to an intercept course and push the engines as hard as they would go, getting in close enough, hopefully, to put a shot across their bow before they could react.

He gave them ten minutes to drift off onto other tasks. No threat from over here, just a dumb-ass country-boy in a small freighter trying to make a quick hit of cash, maybe swapping for useless trinkets from some other poor colony nearby.

It was time.

"All hands, prepare to raise the black flag," he ordered calmly.

Granville had already programmed the course because it needed a good deal of precision, and the target wasn't going to be evading him. He brought the ship around hard and set the engines for maximum burn.

The only thing that went against his instincts right now was not doing a hard ping on their ship, instead relying on their scanner emitters to locate them for him, and hoping they hadn't launched a small shuttle or crew in EVA. He could always rescue someone later, if he needed to, but he wouldn't see them until he was in their laps, as it were.

Apparently, they weren't paying any attention to their screens over on that other bridge. They were sending out a basic navigational ping every sixty seconds, but that was automatic on most vessels in orbit.

And he was accelerating up their asses right now.

"*DYWXK-345029*, this is *PWMGT-6357181*." A

woman's voice now, so the other guy must have gone off duty.

Granville wondered if he had told her anything or if she was frantically looking up comm logs right now.

He ignored her signal. There was nothing she wanted to hear from him, since he was not about to sheer off and apologize for bad piloting.

Sensors detected a hard ping.

Someone had just turned on the big sensor array and sent a pulse at him. Their systems would register that his current course would pass well below and to port from them, which was his plan. Accidents could happen, when ships got too close going too fast.

And he only needed to be close enough to open fire with the Type-3 in the bow.

"*DYWXK-345029*, this is *PWMGT-6357181*. Please respond."

She was growing concerned now. Not quite to the level of red alert and launch the flight wing, but getting there soon.

In twenty seconds, Leomiti would be in range.

"*PWMGT-6357181*, go ahead," he said in a distant, unfocused drawl.

"*DYWXK-345029*, you are violating a no-fly zone and will pass too close on our flank," she snapped. "Sheer off and move to a different orbit, before I notify the authorities and have your pilot's license revoked."

"Negative, *PWMGT-6357181*," Granville let his attention sound like it was wandering. "We're still on course. Have your gyros lost their heading?"

It didn't make any sense, but it didn't have to. He just needed to distract them some more.

"What are you talking about, you idiot?" she demanded. "Heave to. You are a menace to navigation."

The little light on his console went green, indicating that they were hopefully within outer range of the Type-3. He wouldn't know without lighting them up with a targeting scanner, at which point, all hell was likely to break loose.

Granville considered arguing with the woman some more. Maybe rattling her cage pretty hard with a variety of misdirections and profanities, but *Persephone* was really here to drive them to *CS-405*.

It was time for them to get mean.

He pressed the button on his console and brought all the targeting scanners on-line, then he sent a hard pulse of energy downrange from the sensors. It returned quickly, establishing all the baseline parameters he needed as a former fighter jock.

Granville tweaked the course up and in a little bit, like he was shifting into a ramming stance, just to make her choke on her tongue a little extra.

"Bow Gun, put a shot across their bow," he ordered. "You don't have to miss by much, but I want their undivided attention and an undamaged target."

"Roger that, Commander," Leomiti called. "Stand by."

The whole frame of the ship rattled when the gun fired. Lights flickered just the slightest amount as the capacitors dumped and began to suck power out of the generators and batteries. Even the metal vibrated at a slightly different pitch for a moment.

"*DYWXK-345029*, what the hell are you doing?" the woman screamed at him.

Frantic, from the sounds of things.

"We're pirates," Granville growled back. "Surrender or you will be destroyed."

WOLF PACK (JANUARY 4, 403)

Phil considered being angry with the man, but Veitengruber had been following orders, more or less. It was the idiots aboard the other ship that ruined all Phil's carefully laid plans.

Apparently nobody had told them about all the piracy problems over the last eight months. Or they hadn't listened. Something.

Stupid bastards had surrendered instead of running.

He looked down at the console and read the message from Veitengruber again.

Initial assault successful. Vessel has struck. Require assistance in orbit. Persephone.

Then Phil laughed out loud, causing Evan to glance up with a quizzical look.

"Heather, Siobhan, and *Stunt Dude* will be so disappointed," he observed loudly enough to get a round of chuckles from his bridge crew. "They wanted to pull another *Packmule* on this one."

Hard assault against a defended vessel, frantically trying to cover all airlocks as pirates started to hit emergency overrides so they could board. Weasels in the hen house. And instead, the Director over there had apparently rolled over and showed his belly.

Granted, *Persephone* had a big gun, which few small vessels did. That might be enough to overawe civilians in the back end of beyond.

"Send a signal to Heather and Siobhan," Phil continued. "Order them down to orbit at best speed, and then put us in firing range as fast as you can. This signal's nearly three hours old, so things have happened and we need to assist."

Phil caught Evan's nod and then went to work on the next step in the big plan. He almost felt like the dog that had been chasing the car, and then suddenly caught it.

What the hell did they do next?

Trick question. They were the *RAN*. And this was war.

PRISONERS OF WAR (JANUARY 4, 403)

WELL, that hadn't gone according to plan.

Granville studied the gigantic vessel as it lay quiescent in orbit, an elephant he had accidentally, successfully herded, and now had to do something with it.

And nobody was close enough to help, with *CS-405* and the others lying in wait where they expected the vessel to emerge.

He triggered the laser comm and send a quiet plea for help to the upper reaches of this solar system. Three hours and ten minutes until help arrived, best guess.

Those folks would get into too much trouble if he left them alone for that long. He certainly would have, if he was in their boots.

Granville's mind flashed back to the man who had been his first flight instructor, taking a group of rowdy punks and figuring out which half he needed to wash out so that the others turned out to be pilots worth their salt.

When in doubt, audacity.

He programmed a quick escape course into the ship's system for an emergency, and then an even easier plot that someone could engage by just pushing a single button.

"All hands, this Veitengruber," he said unnecessarily into the intercom. He could almost yell loud enough that they could all hear, but he was the only one talking. "Isiah, and Spier, lock down your stations and come forward to the bridge."

Audacity. It was just another word for insanity that happened to turn out to be successful in retrospect. If it failed, he'd probably be dead, so Phil couldn't Court Martial him, and the current plans would be so badly broken that they had to fall back on the alternative.

That might still have been the best option, because the risks just kept getting crazier and riskier.

His two crew members joined him quickly. Granville stood and gestured Isiah to take the right hand crewman's seat in front of him, where the navigator would normally sit. The intercom was still open.

"Isiah, you will continue to maintain Systems from here," he ordered. "Additionally, you will be flying the ship after Spier and I board the enemy vessel."

The young man's head swiveled around like an owl, face gone white, eyes huge and mouth fallen open.

"I have programmed you three course options, Sailor," Granville turned stern. "First one backs you off to a polite distance so you can continue to threaten them with the main gun. Use that unless something bad happens. Second one does the same, but then jumps to where *CS-405* should be waiting."

"And the third?" he asked, filled with dread.

"The third one shuts the entire vessel down by scramming the engines and generators," he replied. "Kam and her crew can probably fix it before the vessel falls out of orbit, but it will take days, so if you get captured, the locals can't do anything except piss Siobhan and Heather off."

"Sir, is this a good idea?" Leomiti's voice joined them like a ghost. "Speaking as senior non-comm present."

And he was. Technically, *Persephone*'s Boatswain, at least until they got a bigger crew and everybody wasn't wearing three hats.

"No," Granville agreed. "It is a terrible idea, but it's the best I've got right now, because we need to put the fear of God into those people immediately, and not in three hours when help arrives. Too much option for mischief."

"And if they capture you, sir?" the young man continued.

"They have struck their colors, Sailor," Granville growled. "If they resist at this point, Imperial regulations allow me to order the vessel annihilated without mercy. Try to kill their bridge, if you have to fire into the vessel. We'll want the engines intact, because we can always use the hull as a troop transport later, even if we have to kill every man and woman aboard. Do I make myself clear?"

Spier and Isiah gulped. Leomiti fell silent. Granville guessed that this was one of those places where Imperial Law differed from Republic, but they were flying an Imperial flag today. And he'd be fine killing everyone over there if push truly came to shove.

This was *Buran*. They did indeed have it coming.

"What about me, sir?" Spier asked in a tiny voice.

"Take the other seat, next to Olshefski," he ordered. "You'll be accompanying me aboard the other vessel, so we'll get personal weapons shortly. For now, just look fierce."

Six minutes had passed since the hospital ship called his bluff by surrendering.

"*PWMGT-6357181*, this is *RAN Persephone*," he opened the line to them again. "We will dock shortly and I will board your vessel to take command. I will remind you that you have surrendered on honorable terms. You will be treated well. If you resist, I have ordered my vessel to stand off and destroy you. Do you understand and accept these terms?"

Blunt, and rather ugly.

Audacity. Six people capturing a civilian vessel with a possible crew of over seven hundred, from the notes he had seen. Walking into the lion's den.

Piece of cake.

"Understood, pirate ship *Persephone*," a man's voice came back. "*The Eldest* will be informed of your behavior and respond accordingly."

Granville highly doubted that, but he wasn't going to say anything out loud. That would be too much like poking a sleeping bear at this point, and he wanted to live through this.

And his hands were only shaking in his mind.

He would have sent Bardeen to open the arms locker, since she was the one not needed right now, but he was the only crew member coded for the lock. It made sense, with a small vessel, that only the Captain and Master of Marines could get to the guns, while on station.

Still it was a pain in his ass, as he felt like he was juggling chainsaws today.

Granville sat and began to plot his approach. The hospital ship wasn't moving, or rather, they were at relative rest, so it was just a case of side-slipping over until he could line up the airlock just aft of the bridge and establish a seal to the other side.

That was when things would get interesting.

His two bridge crew members watched with fascination as he maneuvered in slowly. The Type-3 could still fire while they were docked, but it would be a long, slanted shot if he did. The sort of thing that would damage five or eight chambers to space by slicing the outer hull, like a razor blade opening an orange.

Morgan's gun, on the other hand, would be almost touching their hull when he docked. The splash from firing that close would probably foul the weapon, but the shot might emerge from the other side of the vessel, depending on the chambers and frames it crossed, if he fired it.

Massive damage inflicted, either way. Hopefully, it would never come to that.

The hull rang like a bell as the computer took over for the last ten meters and slid them together, two Lanternfish mating. Hopefully, he could escape his fate later.

Soft seal indicated. Hard seal locked.

Granville was up and racing aft to the arms locker, just this side of the airlock. Spier had followed close behind, which was good. He thumbprinted the lock and handed her a short pulse rifle, while he took a holster and attached it to his thigh, adding a stun pistol a moment later.

She would be using lethal force, but if Able-Spacer Spier had to shoot anything, she would probably be fighting for her life. He could knock down opinionated shits and throw them in the drunk tank until they woke up.

Into the airlock and into a softsuit. They didn't need to attach all the plumbing, as they would only need them in an emergency. Same for not needing the heavier suits that came with some degree of armor.

Police customs inspection, he kept reminding himself.

You're a cop, and they are merchants you only suspect of being smugglers. Keep them occupied until *Stunt Dude* and all his raiders got here.

You can do that.

Granville left the helmet attached to his hip, rather than wearing it. Spier mirrored him. Ten seconds to lock it, if it was an emergency. And there would be no need to do that, right?

Deep breath.

"Isiah, you have the deck until I return or one of the other commanders relieves you," he said aloud. "Cycling the airlock now."

A green light from the bridge indicated that *Persephone*'s second captain had taken command, hopefully temporarily, and was hopefully ready for whatever the next flavor of craziness turned out to be.

Inner side closed and locked. Keypad override so that not even an emergency code could open it. Police vessels were extra paranoid, as he had found.

Granville positioned Spier to his left and back, like a proper escort or bodyguard, and pressed the button on the far side that would open the airlock and let him board the *Buran* vessel.

Another deep breath as the hatch slowly ground its way out into a large chamber.

Four people awaited him. Two were obviously the equivalent of naval marines, but looked like rent-a-cops, considering how fat one was and how slovenly the other appeared. They were there to lend weight to the situation. Neither was armed, which was good.

The important man, on the right, was older, with gray hair buzzed too short, until he looked like a white peach. The wispy mustache trailing down his chin looked comical rather than intimidating. Otherwise, he had the typical Mongolian features of *Buran*, possibly with some Russian thrown in for the ancient *Siberian* look so many of the higher classes cultivated. He appeared frail, but that was just skinniness on his part, as he was standing starkly erect, with an impressive look of distinguished disapproval on his face.

The man also wore classical court robes, rather than something useful on a cattle ranch. Four kimonos were visible, black on the outermost fading to a medium gray closest to his skin.

His Obi was knotted with such precision that Granville figured he must starch it into place each morning after tying it.

The woman next to him was younger. Perhaps forty from the way her long hair was pulled back and showed off salt and pepper stripes. She had green eyes, which was a rarity in a Mongolian face, and a polite smile. Not friendly, but not grinding her teeth in disdain, either.

Unlike the man, she was dressed more comfortably, in what might be surgical scrubs, baggy but covering everything.

"Centurion Veitengruber," he announced simply in Mongolian, foregoing the usual ritual of sharing all names from clan to personal. "Commander of *RAN Persephone*. You are now prisoners under the Recognized Rules of Warfare."

The older man's mouth went sour. The woman continued to observe with a relaxed face. Granville took a deliberate, measured stride across the line in the airlock door to stand before them.

Onto their deck.

The man was tall, but still shorter than Granville was, and the woman was almost petite as he got closer.

"I will see you punished for this criminality," the man snapped.

It would have been a snarl, if there had been any force behind the words, but he appeared to be speaking just to register his disdain for the entire circumstance.

Granville fixed the man with a bored eye and turned to his assistant.

"Seal the airlock, Spier," he ordered in a bureaucratic voice.

She nodded and pressed the obvious button. The door began to beep and then moved a little faster than a glacier. He nodded to her and turned back to the locals.

"Who was formerly in command of this vessel?" Granville asked with his own angry disdain.

Too many years on a cattle ranch came bubbling to the

surface. He would not meet them with meekness, but anger. Polite, but unyielding.

"I am the Director of this vessel," the charming man looked down his nose, which was impressive, being shorter than either of the Imperials.

"Were," Granville corrected him. "There will be a new commander shortly, and you will follow his orders or be subject to Imperial justice."

He gave the man a hard, challenging look as he spoke, hoping the man would do something stupid. Granville had disliked him at first sight and didn't see that changing as they got to know one another. There was always a brig somewhere, probably aboard *CS-405*, if the fool pressed his luck while standing on thin ice.

To add insult to injury, Granville ignored the man now, concentrating his attention on the woman. He gave her a polite, formal, half-bow, as one might when encountering a stranger of unknown station. If one had spent seven years in *The Holding* learning such things.

Even on a cattle ranch.

The tiny gasp that escaped her mouth told him that he had done it correctly.

"And you would be?" Granville's tones became polite and almost endearing.

Bad cop, good cop.

"Au Aqal Corven Sam," she replied with her own correct bow. "Chief Medical Officer aboard *PWMGT-6357181*."

Her voice had a lovely lilt, somewhere in the high alto range, and she knew how to use it as an instrument. Granville suspected she had received vocal music training at some point. He had known many Imperial women with similar skills.

Granville nodded and smiled.

"Why was this act necessary?" she continued, dancing precisely and lightly around the possible edges of correctness in such a situation.

Not challenging his *fait accompli*, nor his *force majeure*, but wishing merely to receive enlightenment. Obviously, the woman was a Scholar, which would help. The man struck Granville as a Warrior who had retired from active naval service and taken up civilian tasks.

Granville stared once around the room, but the six of them were the only people present. It was a white room, painted recently, from the hints of the smell still in the air. The floor showed a few scuffs, but nothing like regular traffic to dull the shine of the metal.

Even the walls had been cleaned up, with all the suits he would have normally expected having been moved somewhere else. Probably stashed in a storage closet when company arrived unexpectedly. The pegs and frames on the walls where they would have hung looked bare.

At least the air was sweeter here. He had to agree with Isiah about adding a greenhouse room to the hydroponics. Too many years around cattle had apparently dulled his smell, but the sudden tang made it clear.

He made a mental note to address that when he got home, while seeking the words for Doctor Sam Au's question.

Why was this act necessary?

When in doubt, audacity.

"We are on a mercy mission, madam," he said simply.

"My squadron's next mission is to raid one of *The Holding*'s prison planets and rescue as many Imperial citizens as we can, in order to take them home."

The man wanted to snarl something into the conversation at this point. Granville scowled at him. From behind, Spier had apparently stepped back and to one side, possibly pointing the carbine suddenly.

Dr. Sam Au put a hand on the older man's wrist and directed her own interruption.

"This is a civilian hospital vessel, Centurion," Sam Au said carefully.

"And some of those men may have been there for forty years, Doctor," he replied. "*The Eldest* has never returned a single prisoner taken by your fleets, in a war that has lasted several decades."

He caught the faintest blush on her face, but Au's attention was focused on the Director, keeping him from saying something that would probably get him shot right now.

The two security men looked nervously alert, but not like they were preparing for action. In his mind, Granville downgraded them to movie theater ushers, missing only the tacky fringe on their shoulder boards to complete the costume.

Just to be extra intimidating, Granville scowled at the two of them as well and made a show of unhooking the little strap of leather holding the pistol in his holster. The fat one blanched.

"And if we were to refuse to assist?" she asked in an oblique, intellectual way that contained not a single gram of threat or emotion.

"The man who has been tasked with taking over as Director of this vessel is a trained nurse from *Aquitaine*," Granville gave her a frigid smile. "He is also a naval officer with very well developed opinions on the ancient Hippocratic Oath all of our physicians take in order to practice medicine and its bearing to this situation. Do you still take that Oath?"

"Something very similar, if my studies were correct, Centurion," the woman said.

"Then I might reconsider approaching the topic with any negativity on your part."

"Or else what?" the former Director's temper finally got the better of him.

"Personally, I would just dump you onto the planet below us in lifepods," Granville sneered. "We have no interest in taking slaves, unlike *The Holding*."

"Slaves?" he raged, still carefully not moving even a millimeter that might be interpreted as provocation. "How dare you?"

"I was captured at *Samara*, seven years ago," Granville felt his face and voice harden in equal increments. "My life since then was chattel slavery on a cattle ranch on a planet you've probably never heard of, not all that far from here, and just like the one below you. You can help us, or become a problem that must be resolved. I look forward to solving it."

His tone left no doubts as to what his vote would be.

"I just want the hull, so we can get all of our people home," Granville continued to grind out the words harshly. "You can fulfill your oath and help, or forget what it means to be human, and become friction. Hopefully,

Admiral Kosnett will take an even harsher view of you than I might."

Granville fell silent and watched. The two ushers looked like they wanted to turn invisible and flee. The man subsided when the woman touched his arm again, just a gentle reminder that looked like she was in charge here, and he was just the pilot.

Doctor Au studied Granville's face closely for a second.

"Understand that the ship's permanent crew is differentiated from the medical staff aboard?" she asked carefully, still a Scholar looking for a simple answer, rather than a Warrior set to apply violence to all actions.

Granville had been raised and trained as the equivalent of a Warrior, before he knew who these people were, but he was also an officer and a gentleman, *By Order of His Sovereign Majesty Karl VII, Emperor of Fribourg by Grace of God.*

"So noted," Granville responded.

"I command both sides of the equation," she continued. "But the responses will be different."

"I am happy to send your troublemakers down to the planet right now," Granville smiled frostily at her. "And while I cannot speak for the Admiral himself, I am aware of other prisoners who have been taken by our squadron, who have been treated well, and who will be released without restrictions once the current operation is completed."

"The *Fribourg Empire* is not known for its honor, Centurion," Sam Au said carefully, almost testing his resolve.

"That is because you people are fools, Doctor."

Among the educated classes, such language was just about as insulting as one could manage. Her eyes widened and her cheeks blushed furiously. The man beside her flinched, but remained perfectly still as Granville's hand fell to the holster again.

Rather than let things get further out of hand, Granville squared his shoulders and stood tall.

"Take me to the bridge," he ordered. "Let us begin the process of organizing things so that when the rest of my people arrive, we look professional."

She nodded. The man almost growled, but held his peace.

She dismissed the two goons to their quarters with strict instructions and threats of punishment, so Granville let them go. The man led, with her following and Granville and Spier trailing.

The bridge of the hospital ship was forward, rather than aft like on *Packmule*, but the interior was very similar. One Director's station on his raised dais facing the rest. Half a dozen stations for lesser beings to sit while worshipping the man. Ugly, white walls, too bright for normal operations or sanity.

Hushed voices and six people scurrying to their feet as their former Director entered. Four female, two male, reminding him that this was also not *Fribourg*.

Granville strode to the center of the room and turned in place once to frame everyone's attention.

"I will not be your new Director," he said simply. "I will not be the head of the security team that will take possession of this vessel and its crew shortly. You may think of me as the avenging angel who will come for your very souls if anything happens to one of my people."

He paused and scanned faces. Not much outright hostility. Mostly utter shock, and that wasn't going to wear off all that quickly.

"I was a prisoner on a *Holding* world until very recently," he continued. "My mission today is to rescue more slaves and get them home. You can decide you don't wish to help us, and I will vote to deliver you to the planet below. Those that stay will be treated like crew until they give me a reason to think otherwise. At the end of the mission, I expect the Director in charge to send all of you home, quite possibly aboard this very ship, if that is an option. Who is in charge of security?"

All eyes turned to a mousy woman in the center of the group.

"How big is your team?" he asked starkly.

This was their first challenge. They had surrendered, but only to barbarians, and lies told to those people didn't count.

Except Granville Veitengruber was speaking accentless Mongolian to them. And carrying himself like a Warrior. Old socialization patterns would activate.

"Nineteen," she said warily. "With a ship's crew of eighty-one and two hundred seventeen medical staff aboard."

Granville nodded at her.

"Should I arrange to have the nineteen sent to the surface immediately?" he asked.

Interestingly, the security woman's eyes went to Dr.

Au, rather than the Director with no name. Granville watched the silent byplay.

"Treated well and sent home afterwards?" she clarified.

"We have other prisoners already who will be," he said flatly. "The *Fribourg Empire* is more civilized than *The Holding* in that regard."

Another blush. Nobody liked being lectured by barbarians about their own supposed shortcomings. Especially not ethical ones, in a society that claimed to exemplify the highest ethical standards possible.

"There are perhaps a handful that would bear watching," she said carefully. "With a like number of standard crew, as well."

"You and I will talk later," he replied carefully. "With Dr. Au present. I would rather eliminate temptation and let the planet have the troublemakers now with my apologies, rather than have to kill the entire crew while putting down any attempt at mutiny."

Every face went white at those words. As he had intended.

Carrot. Stick.

On *Abakn*, his choice had been to work, or starve. *Mansi* was probably the same, with the added benefit of no trade or resupply, except what the wardens in their kremlin allowed.

Let these fine folks know that they had choices. Rats will flee violence, as long as they can. It was only when cornered that they got dangerous.

"Who flies this vessel?" he asked the group.

"I am the Pilot," the man with no name snapped.

"You were the Director of ship-side," Granville

corrected. "I doubt you calculated orbits and drift. And you will be silent or I will stuff you into a lifepod right now and let the planet have you."

One of the men raised his hand quaintly.

"I was in charge of flight operations, Your Grace," he said meekly.

"Do you wish to continue?" Granville asked.

The man shrugged.

"Yes, Your Grace," he finally said.

"Good," Granville decided, pointing. "Everyone to your stations. Dr. Au, you two over there, watched by Spier. Comm officer, open a channel to *Persephone*. Put it on conference mode for everyone to hear."

A moment of frightened stillness, and then bodies exploded into motion, watching screens and pressing buttons.

"Uhm, *Persephone* here," Isiah's voice came back unsteadily.

"Veitengruber, checking in," he said. "Back off to a safe distance and continue your watch, Sailor. I might be sending lifepods to the surface, so tell the gunners to ignore them. I will clear with you before we send a shuttle."

Silent threat: we might have blown them up, like uncivilized people. Or captured them in the act of trying to escape. Obvious carrot: jumping into a pod now would get you safely away from the pirates. Marooned here, but safe.

Granville just hoped there was a big enough cattle ranch below to take them all to, so they might get a chance to experience the utter hell that had been his life for many years, but he had a small soul.

"Roger that, sir," Isiah replied.

"The line is dead, Director," a tall, redheaded woman on the far left said nervously.

"Correct," Granville replied. "Message delivered. Our cultures are different."

"Yes, sir," she said.

"Nav officer, *Persephone* will be detaching from our airlock on autopilot and moving to an escort position off our port flank," he announced. "Maintain your current course, elevation, heading, and status until ordered otherwise."

"Yes, Your Grace," the man looked up and nodded, focused intently on doing absolutely nothing. And doing it well.

Granville turned to Dr. Au and her sidekick. He smiled at the man.

"Would you like a lifepod now?" Granville asked. "Or should we wait until I have enough crew picked out to fly you all down in the administrative shuttle?"

"I will depart with my loyal crew," the man snapped, still carefully not gesturing.

"Good enough," Granville said. "Security officer, take Spier with you and place this man in a holding cell or isolated cabin. Lock down all communications to isolate him further, and then notify the kitchen to deliver meals to the chamber when the rest of the crew is fed."

"Acknowledged, sir," the woman stood again.

She gestured politely to Spier, and less so to the old

man, moving them back out of the chamber and leaving him alone with Sam Au and the bridge crew.

"Now what?" the Doctor asked after the room had fallen to silence.

"Now we wait," he said. "My support team will arrive shortly and we will reorganize things more fully."

"The administrative shuttles can hold eighteen each," she offered.

"Then hopefully, we will only need one flight," Granville answered. "I would like to think that most of you have some level of human compassion left in you."

He made a note of which faces smiled, which blushed, and which scowled. Right now, it was him against the entire crew.

CLEANUP CREW (JANUARY 4, 403)

Trinidad nearly laughed out loud.

"I can't believe he went and did this to me," he heard Siobhan grumble again under her breath, as the two of them were looking out *Anna*'s cockpit window at the big hospital ship, trailing like a little remora. One of *405*'s shuttles was just about to undock from the primary airlock, and then it would be their turn.

"You're upset?" *Stunt Dude* replied, grinning. "I was all set to pull off a boarding action to make *Packmule* look tame. Then he goes and gets them to surrender instead of running off to where we could ambush them."

That brought a small smile to her face, after the scowls. She had been there with him.

Capturing *Packmule* in deep space had been the most insane thing ever. Blink-jumping *Anna* across six light-seconds. Free jumping across deep space. Latching on and boarding them secretly in the middle of nowhere.

Taking a fleeing hospital in deep space would have been another level of crazy for the books.

The other shuttle finished its task and backed away finally.

He watched Siobhan maneuver in, lining things up and establishing a hardlock so the airlock doors could open.

"All yours," she said, but *Stunt Dude* was already gone, out of his chair with a wave and down the stairs. Down in the hall, bodies were packed too tightly to move, but only aft of the airlock, with everybody down in the cargo hold and lined up on the stairs.

"Open her up," Trinidad ordered as he spotted Nakisha at the lock door.

He joined her a moment later as the hatch began to beep.

Vlad greeted them on the other side, part of the earlier team from *CS-405* that had boarded.

"All clear, *Stunt Dude*," he said with a grin.

"Roger that," Trinidad replied.

There was one of the other ship's crew standing next to Vlad nervously. She was tiny, compared to the big marine, and looked a little overwhelmed.

"Take this man to the bridge," Vlad said slowly and carefully. His accent was bad, but the words were clear enough.

She bobbed her head to Vlad, then to Trinidad, and then scampered forward.

Trinidad turned back after three steps.

"Nakisha, with me," he said. "The rest of you line up

with previous teams and take over watches. Engineering folks stay especially alert for saboteurs."

Assents, and then he was moving forward, trailing the small woman who kept stopping to look back and make sure he was with her as they went forward and up.

The bridge looked almost like a mirror of Packmule when they got there. Maybe a little larger, befitting a bigger crew, but the same otherwise. Able-Spacer Spier was standing guard, but the only others in the room were existing crew. They were nervously twitchy, but not dangerous, except perhaps to themselves.

"Where's Granville?" he asked as his escort stood to one side, rocking her weight back and forth.

"Forward conference room B-2," Spier said, directing her words to the crewwoman. "Please deliver this man to the Director."

Again, the bobbing nod and churning feet. Trinidad had to stretch his legs to keep up as she went back the way they had come, stopping at about twenty meters up the hallway and standing to one side as she opened a hatch, bowing at the waist.

These folks were a little too much, as near as he could tell, but apparently Veitengruber had put a genuine fear of God himself into them, which was impressive, since they only worshipped *Buran*.

Inside, he found Granville and Andre, along with Kam and an incredibly attractive local woman who seemed to just float atop of all the madness that had infected the rest of the crew.

"*Stunt Dude*, this is Doctor Au Aqal Corven Sam," Granville said as he and Nakisha entered.

She rose with as much grace as she had beauty.

"*Stunt Dude?*" she asked, holding her hand out.

"Centurion Trinidad Mildon," he corrected with a smile. "Security Chief of *CS-405* and *Task Force Barnaul*. The crew occasionally refer to me as *Stunt Dude*, due to a previous career working in movies."

"I see," she nodded, perhaps with a twinkle in her eyes.

They sat, him across from the doctor and close enough to Andre Gave to feel the man's nervous tension.

"So I've already basically arrested and quarantined the original Director," Veitengruber began as he and Nakisha sat down. "He was going to be a pain in Andre's ass, any way we went, and it wasn't worth it. I've also suggested to Dr. Au and the local head of security that we identify the other dozen or so troublemakers and send them all to the ground, right now. Thoughts?"

"Is the number going to be that small?" Trinidad fired back, studying the woman's face for clues. "Do we dump the entire ship's crew and stock with our own people? Once we leave, the options come down to locking them in cabins or spacing them."

Not that he would, but if they thought that was an option, he figured they'd be nicer to Andre on the way. Once he had a chance to interview some of them, they'd know if these folks were safe with Imperials.

She blushed. Hard. In a cute way. The bones in her face were broad and almost flat, but the shoulders were narrow, making her head look almost oversized.

"You act like we're barbarians," she tried to counter.

"You are," Veitengruber snarled. "At least until proven otherwise. I've lived among you for many years."

Deeper blush this time. Went all the way down her neck and vanished under her top.

"Some of the crew will likely be a problem, yes," she agreed, demure and careful. "I won't dispute that, and I'm sure we can identify them and safely remove them now, rather than resorting to extreme measures. This is a hospital ship."

"How much gerontology experience does your staff have?" Andre spoke up suddenly.

The man's voice had gone from the normal, almost whine Trinidad had listened to for the last three weeks, into a deeper, more focused tone. This was Andre before *Packmule*, when he was just a nurse having to deal with even-more-whiny patients with the sniffles.

Firm. Stubborn. Intense.

"Some," Dr. Au's eyes got a little flittery, blinking too rapidly and shuttling back and forth as she accessed mental files.

"All of your patients will be men," Andre's suddenly-implacable voice rang. "Between the ages of young adult and dead from old age. I expect they have had some access to their medical personnel, but almost no medicines or advanced technology. We do not know how many there are, nor how many we can transport. What is the bed count on your ship?"

That seemed to stabilize her. Get to the technical side of things. The eyes focused on Andre, ignoring him, Nakisha, and Veitengruber, all of whom she probably saw as bad cops.

As she should.

"We are configured for one thousand, two hundred

patients at present," she said, her voice losing some of the ragged edges. "With four surgical theaters. The Lander also contains six surgical theaters and recovery facilities, plus two dentists. In a catastrophe, we can break out enough beds to handle three thousand patients for a short period."

"This will be longer, Doctor Au," Andre said. "From our target, the plan is to return to Imperial space as close to directly as we can, but that will still take weeks of sailing to reach the closest fleet base. How seriously do you and your people take your Hippocratic Oath?"

That last question sounded almost like a biblical patriarch, seeing the Face of God and forever changed.

"At least as seriously as you," she challenged.

"That's on your head, Doctor," Andre said simply. "I've already treated several citizens of *The Holding*. All of them are in excellent health and will return to their own lives when we're done here."

Her chin came up, almost defiantly. Trinidad wasn't smitten, but damn, was she cute when she did that.

"If they are prisoners of war, then they attacked one of our worlds and were captured in the process," she stated.

"No," Veitengruber rumbled ominously.

She turned to face him, eyes growing hot.

"No?" she asked tartly, emotion starting to get the better of her.

"The ship I command was formerly a police cutter in Imperial Service," Veitengruber ground out the words like a blacksmith pounding red hot steel. "Those ships do not serve with fleets, but protect Imperial worlds. They are customs enforcers for internal security. There were six of them at the junkyard we raided. All of those were taken from Imperial space by your warships raiding our systems. Your hands are not clean, Doctor."

And, back to the blush. Trinidad decided to derail things, before the emotions got fully out of control.

"So we're here," he said, leaning forward. "We're going somewhere else and picking up a bunch of old and possibly broken men, so we can take them home. Are your people going to help, or hinder? Their ransom is on your head, Doctor Au."

Those pretty green eyes narrowed as she focused on him. Trinidad smiled the kind of smile a dragoon like him practiced in the mirror, for dealing with new marines, fresh out of boot camp, who thought they were all that.

Long pause this time. Maybe finally paying attention. Doing the math in her head.

"Most of them will be doctors and nurses first, and patriots second," she said. "The Centurion has already identified the ship's Director, Ro Calla Dyen Mak, as a probable instigator. A few others will probably be too sullen to count. Possibly three of the nineteen security forces."

"Only three?" Trinidad asked. "That seems low."

"These are not Warriors, *Stunt Dude*," she countered, softening finally. "When we land on the surface of a planet, they keep watch on equipment, and check identities at portals. Most of them are probably more comfortable helping little, old ladies across the street, to quote the ancient saying. That is why I hire them. Ship's crew is a different group, as they are permanently attached to the hull and under Director Ro. I hire everyone else. They answer to me."

"And you will answer to me," Andre Gave, *Ancient Prophet*, said. "I will command this vessel and this crew. The Dragoon will answer to me. Your people will answer to me. We are on a mercy mission here, but at the end of the day, we are all human, and I will expect them to display human empathy."

"And when all of this is done?" she turned to Andre. It was like a spotlight in Trinidad's face had gone out. "What then? We will be deep behind enemy lines and prisoners. What guarantees do we have that the tables will not be reversed, with my crew kept in prisons for the rest of their lives?"

"I will personally escort you to the border, Doctor," Veitengruber replied. "Load our crew onto my vessel, and send the rest of you home. My word as a Gentleman and Imperial officer."

"And if your superiors do not agree?" she snapped.

Trinidad couldn't remember ever seeing Veitengruber actually smile. Scowl a lot. Pensive most of the time. Angry, like now.

But he was smiling. And that smile turned to encompass the rest of them.

"Then I guess we'll have to stage a jailbreak," he said. "We are pirates, after all."

Trinidad grinned back and nodded.

PREPARATION (JANUARY 27, 403)

ANDRE WAS on the bridge of the ship Phil had renamed *RAN Forgotten Mercy*. There was already an *RAN Mercy* in Republic service, somewhere. Idly, Andre wondered if he really wanted to move up and command it, one of these days. The last three weeks had been an even greater crash course than service on *Packmule* with Heather.

Here, he was in charge. All the fuck-ups were his to own.

Nothing like possibly getting Court Martialed for doing something wrong aboard a ship you stole from someone else fair and square.

At least they were home. Or as home as *Lighthouse Station* could be.

"Gan," Andre called out. "What's the neighborhood look like?"

Andre wasn't the least bit interested in the whole four-name-in-reverse thing that *Buran* did to name and socialize people. After three days, he called them all by their personal name. Easier that way.

"We're last in, Andre," the woman replied, also comfortable enough not to call him Director first. "Flagship is in high orbit. *Packmule* is lower. The other two have already landed on the planet below. Permission to send out a ping?"

"Granted," Andre said. "One, just so you can put us into a parking orbit not far from *Packmule*. And can you put the current image of the planet on the main screen, please? Comm, send our compliments to the flagship and tell them we'll be in place shortly."

Andre poked around on the buttons on his right hand armrest until he found the one he wanted. Why did the intercom have to be hard-wired? And why didn't the Director of a ship like this have his own console to call up data? Even *Packmule* had been that civilized.

Then he remembered the man they had sent to *Kyzyl's* surface. Men, and women, including that one long-time prisoner they had taken at *Abakn*, just to make things crazier. That look of angry disdain for having his own ship stolen by a bunch of pirates.

Yeah, that was a man who never got his own hands dirty.

Briefly, Andre considered asking one of the engineers to run a screen in here. Maybe pull out the damned dais and throne, and replace them with a standard station, like everyone else in here used.

"Doctor Au," he said into the comm. "Could you join me on the bridge, please?"

He closed the line and located the woman in charge

of the flight deck. This beast was only technically a carrier, with that big hospital lander's dock taking up most of the forward third of the ship. Just aft of it were three admin shuttles. They were smaller than Republic versions, designed mostly as trucks to haul a few people and a dozen cubic meters of supplies between orbit and ground.

"Ross, tell *Stunt Dude* to have the pilots ready," Andre ordered.

"Yes, sir," she barely glanced up and nodded, going back to her screens.

Too risky to ask the locals to fly one of the shuttles here. Too much temptation. But they were designed to be flyable by almost anyone, so parking them just outside and docking to one of the airlocks to free up the decks would only tie up three security folks for an hour or so. And then *Saddlebags* could arrive with the first supply run.

The hatch opened and the woman doctor entered.

She had relaxed some in the time of her pirate adventure. Andre guessed she was a pretty easy-going person normally, so she had eventually taken all this in stride, rather than becoming a harridan, like the Director Ro would have.

She smiled and took up a spot on his right, facing the screen on the wall.

"So this is *Lighthouse Station*?" she asked carefully.

She asked everything carefully. Andre wondered if that was a Scholar thing or if she was nervous that someone like *Stunt Dude* would overreact.

He laughed inside. Nobody knew where this was, because he had personally programmed the jumps each time, from Heather's notes. Andre Gave, Nurse and bad-ass Astrogator.

And certainly, Granville and Trinidad had worked hard to frighten the crew with deliberate brutality on day one, just so every day after that was a nicer place, and people would hopefully keep their juvenile delinquency tendencies to themselves.

"It is," Andre said. "We stole a herd of cattle and every chicken we could lay hands on, on one of our raids. Put them all down there and have been collecting milk and eggs."

"How do you store them?" her face grew confused.

"As pasta and hardtack bread," he smiled. "It may not be all that exciting, but we captured megatons of wheat on *Packmule*, and *405*'s got the best cook I've ever known in the service."

"At a secret base behind enemy lines?" she asked. There was a tease in her voice now that was an improvement.

Andre was one of only three people who could unlock the JumpDrive controls. If something happened to him, Trinidad, and Nakisha, the ship would be trapped in deep space forever.

"We'll probably abandon it after this," he said. "Turn the horses and cattle out to go feral. Keep the chickens, though. We want to go home."

"So it's not a colony?" She was still confused.

They hadn't gone too much into detail, until now. Just sailed.

"We actually considered asking our first pair of prisoners if they knew people in *The Holding* we could recruit to run the place," Andre laughed. "But that was just too complicated a swindle to pull off in the time we had."

"For an enemy fleet supposedly filled with Warriors, Andre, you people seem to be con artists," Sam Au replied lightly.

She seemed to be back on stable ground. It helped that she understood what they were doing. Never assume the enemy is the enemy, until pushed.

It also helped that three other ships had guns, in case the crew here got restive. Andre had originally figured he had a one in three chance of a Viking funeral when he came aboard *Forgotten Mercy*.

"Pirates," he corrected her with a smile. "You have not met the woman who started all this. Centurion Siobhan Skokomish is nominally Second Officer aboard *CS-405*, but she has earned the nickname *Lady Blackbeard*, after the ancient pirate."

"And yet, your squadron is part of Keller's force," she said, giving name to the terrible monster coming for their souls.

"Indeed," Andre said. "But we got separated after a raid when the ship's Jump engines broke down. By the time we fixed it, Phil Kosnett had decided that piracy was the best way to continue our mission to harry and damage *The Holding*. At least until they sued for terms and maybe we could have peace."

"All nations must bow to *Buran*," she quoted something, probably a childhood admonition.

It didn't have any emotion behind it, so he presumed it was just a saying, and not a belief.

"No," Andre said simply, watching the six heads in

front of him trying to surreptitiously listen to the conversation.

"No?" she continued. "It is the destiny of all mankind to be united into a common whole, for the good of all humans."

"*Buran* keeps slaves, Sam," Andre felt his voice grow heavier. *Meaner.* "Veitengruber was stuck on the same cattle ranch as we stole all the cows from. The place we are going to is a prison world without parole. When the Empire and the Republic warred, prisoners were traded home on a regular and almost formal basis, without restrictions. And our children are free to choose their own lives, rather than being placed into a caste for the rest of their lives. I chose to be a nurse."

She shook her head. It wasn't negation, but some internal monolog. He had been pounding on her every chance he got for three weeks, just because he couldn't imagine anybody as smart and empathic as Sam Au wouldn't be moved by those arguments.

At least three of the primary bridge crew in front of him had been. Andre suspected several defections and asylum claims when they got to Imperial space.

Assuming they survived that long.

Nurse, astrogator, and revolutionary?

Not bad, if he did say so himself. Kermit would never hear the end of it, once he got back to *CS-405* permanently.

A tiny voice emerged from the woman now.

"I would like to see this *Lighthouse Station*?" she asked.

Andre gave in and listened to the evil conscience on his left shoulder.

"I believe Director Kosnett would probably approve a field trip," he said, louder than necessary, in case somebody *wasn't* eavesdropping. "Perhaps others would like to go down with us to see?"

Four heads popped up and made eye contact at that. Several included the faintest of nods in his direction.

"Po," Andre turned to the guy on his far right. "Signal to the flagship. Brevet Command Centurion Gave asking permission to take the command crew of *RAN Forgotten Mercy* on a field trip to the surface. I'm pretty sure we can all fit into one of the shuttles, or maybe two if we throw in some marines to make it look like we're not stealing anything."

Snickers echoed back from faces suddenly looking down at screens again. Andre had been enlightening all of them for three weeks. Even if Director Ro came back eventually, he'd be eyeballs deep in comic insubordination as he tried to inflict his authority on people used to Andre being in command.

"You're serious," Sam stated, eyes wide and huge.

"Yes, I am, Doctor," he replied. "We are not barbarians. Personally, most of us consider you people to be evil, but that's just because we're free, and that's what your immortal OverGod wants to take away from us. He wants to impose his will on the entire galaxy, but this is a creature who chose to bombard an inhabited world without any provocation, killing millions of innocent souls. That same galaxy will never forget that there are some evils too great to accept."

Great, add ethical philosopher to the *curriculum vitae? What the hell are you turning into, Nurse?*

Bok tried to keep his face neutral as he watched the two shuttles unload. Tourists were probably necessary, but it didn't mean he had to like it. Still, Kosnett had given his approval, so Bok had to at least pretend to be civil.

He dismounted and tied the roan mare to the post near some hay. She'd stay put for now, and even if she got frisky, the yard was penned enough that she would just dance around outside of reach until she finally got hungry. Or tired of all the noisy people running around.

Nurse Gave, plus the Dragoon and two others, were escorting seven unarmed civilians down from the new hospital ship. He walked over with a deliberate stride, fixing his eyes on the woman between Andre and Trinidad. She looked like she was in charge.

"Boatswain," Trinidad nodded as he got close.

"Welcome," Bok replied, even if they weren't. "We're a mite busy today, so we can do a quick tour of some things, and then dinner will start serving in about an hour, and we can join them then."

"Bok Battenhouse, this is Sam Au, Chief Medical Officer from the new ship, *Forgotten Mercy*," Andre introduced the woman first, and then pointed to the group arrayed behind them. "Kav, Po, Gan, Ross, Mer, and Lin."

The tiny woman shook his hand like equals, while the others all bowed to some extent or other. He hadn't changed into anything formal for this, staying in the heavy canvas dungarees and matching jacket, both done in fleet green.

She turned and it looked like she was sniffing the air around them. Luckily, they were more or less upwind of the chickens right now, so the primary smell was cow shit, mixed in with a healthy dollop of ozone from the welding happening over on the other end of the field, where *Persephone* was landed and getting all the new armaments.

"What's that?" she asked, pointing at the six stainless steel tanks sitting next to the barn.

"Milk," Bok replied simply, still feeling out who this person was. "We load it on the right and process it slowly to the left. Some of it gets powdered for long-term storage. Most of the last few weeks of supply have been turned into butter, and *Saddlebags* will be hauling it all up to *CS-405* and *Forgotten Mercy* as soon as the first tanker is ready."

"Real, raw milk?" she sounded concerned. Possibly insulted.

"The gene for processing cow's milk is extremely common in the Empire, Doctor," he replied. "Most of the men we rescue will be able to drink milk. It is a very good way to get them hydrated and put fat into their system, on the assumption that they're probably all relatively undernourished. If your folks don't want any, that just means more for the rest. Julius will enjoy having more milk solids to make creams, gravies, and alfredos from."

"Your cook?" she asked.

"*CS-405*'s Master of the Wardroom, yes," Bok agreed.

He wondered why the others were staying silent and just watching, but this little woman wasn't intimidating. She was just a medical doctor.

"And you really intend to just abandon all this when you're done here?" she asked, gesturing at the barn, the house, the tanks, the fields, and even the dry-dock with one arm.

Bok shrugged.

"We'll have done what we needed," he replied. "Unless the war ends tomorrow, we're too far away from friendly trade, although one of my people has decided that she wants to file a petition with the Imperial Court to be granted the world on *Letters Patent*."

"Who?" Trinidad spoke up with a curious scowl.

"Avelina's got delusions," Bok chuckled.

The others joined in, if a touch nervously, afraid of not participating, perhaps. Strangers in strange lands.

"Is that possible, sir?" the woman doctor asked.

He shrugged again. This was one of the reasons he never wanted to be an officer. Too much work.

"Worst the Emperor can do is say no," he offered. "If the war does end, she's got a reasonable claim and sweat equity, assuming *Buran* doesn't just show up like pirates and take over."

My, that seemed to get a bigger response out of the doctor than it should have. Sensitive spot?

Bok heard a sudden clomp come up behind him, and then *someone* was slobbering on his arm, sticking her nose around to find the pocket where he kept carrots.

He reached back and grabbed the reins she had pulled loose from the rail before she could escape. He gave the horse a stern look. Not that she cared. There might be carrots.

The others had all stepped back, some of them looking utterly terrified of the big dope.

"She's harmless," he said to the group. "Wants a carrot."

He dug into the inner pocket of his jacket and pulled one out. They grew like weeds in this valley once he had planted them. And the horses were in heaven.

The doctor was less frightened than the rest, so he handed the carrot to her.

"She won't bite, but hold it out with your fingertips or she'll slobber all over your hand," he intoned.

The little doctor did, almost like a mouse placating a cat. The roan mare rotated her head in excitement, and reached out with dainty lips to steal the carrot away before anybody could stop her.

She was a dork, sometimes.

A happily-munching dork.

"Tame," the woman said in surprise.

"Smarter than dogs, generally," Bok replied. "I have to use a lock to hold her pen closed, because she figured out how to unwind the length of wire I had been using. Came out to find her curled up in the feed hay, snoring. But pretty harmless. Wanted to see the strangers, and maybe steal a carrot. And she won't be satisfied just watching."

He turned and mounted back up into the saddle, waiting for the inevitable wiggle as she got her butt settled just right under his weight. Predictable as sunrise.

Bok turned the mare's head in the direction of the chicken coops and tapped her with a heel. She really didn't like the birds all that much, too smelly and opinionated, even for a horse, but she wanted to see *PEOPLE*.

"Shall we?" he called as she walked over with her usual jaunty stride.

He watched the rest follow at a safe distance, so now he was a park ranger giving tours to city folks. At least it would keep her as entertained as it did them. Not like he was going to get any real work done today.

BUILDING THE MANTICORE (JANUARY 29, 403)

THE GROUP from orbit was a mixed bag, but Bok seemed to have them well in hand, so Siobhan didn't bother stopping what she was doing.

"What's all that?" Granville emerged from the innards of *Persephone* into the afternoon sun, shading his eyes to peer at *Stunt Dude*'s tour group across the landing field.

"Andre and *Stunt Dude*," Siobhan answered. "The Chief Medical Officer off the new ship wanted to see the ranch and Phil agreed. Apparently several more folks joined in."

"We worried about spies?" he asked.

"That's why *Stunt Dude*, Bok, and Nakisha have them in hand," Siobhan grinned grimly. "Not like they know where they are, and we'll be gone soon enough."

He nodded and leaned over to inspect the work she was doing. Not that it required much.

Markus and Galin had been busy with the overhead crane. They would pull a missile tube into place and then spot weld it enough to hold when they let go. Then a second team would come along and take the time to put solid welds everywhere that would hold up against JumpSpace and firing.

Her job was locating the closest control access plug to any tube and unscrewing all the bolts so it could open, after which a wiring team could connect the missile's controls to a launch panel on the bridge.

Only when all that was done would they take the time to actually load the bulky missiles up and test the electronics. Three days, maybe.

"Is this going to work?" Granville asked in a low voice.

Not that there was anybody around, but he was speaking quietly.

"Which part?" Siobhan asked, letting her own voice drift down.

Seriously, nobody was within ten meters, and the crane overhead beeped when it moved and howled when it coiled, so nobody was listening.

"Can I just sail right up to a station and blast it out of existence?" Granville asked.

She heard the apprehension in his voice. Not outright terror. More like a fear of screwing up when his people were counting on him.

Not that she'd ever been there.

"Lemme tell you about Alber' d'Maine," she said with a warming smile. "He's commanding an Expeditionary Cruiser these days. *RAN VI Victrix*. But the stories about his craziness go back way before that, to when he was on *Shivaji*, or even old *Rajput*. He does this sort of thing as a matter of course. The big guns on *VI Victrix* are Type-4 beams, rather than Primaries."

"Wait," Granville said. "Type-4's? That's insane."

"Long story," Siobhan replied. "Has to do with space efficiency and long-tail logistics issues. Anyway, he's come out of Jump at full speed and been on top of a station with those guns before they had time to get their power absorber panels fully charged. Our last raid, just before all this, was at *Severnaya Zemlya*. *II Augusta*'s Fast Strike Bombers came out of Jump, fired right into the hull, and then leapt clear. Rest of the squadron came down on them like an avalanche, blasting with everything we had, including the little Type-1-Pulse guns on *405*. We only didn't get away because something broke in JumpSpace and cooked both sets of sails as we got to the edge of the system. But Jessica Keller's First Expeditionary Fleet is known for this sort of thing. You can do it, too. You're one of us now."

"And if it fails?" he asked. "If I fail?"

"We're wiring it all up and hopefully it works," Siobhan said. "Worst case, you get captured again and the rest of us have to go home and grab a major warfleet to bust you out. I know Heather and Phil would be all over that, even if they had to go all the way back to *Ladaux* to get the people."

"But I'm still an Imperial officer, Siobhan," he said, obviously pained.

"We all are, these days, Granvie," she teased lightly. "And you took an Oath to the *RAN*, to go with your other one. We don't leave people behind."

"Just like that?" he asked, voice still soft and a little nervous.

"Just like that, my friend," she told him. "Those are your friends down there. Watching the sky every night and hoping that one of these days they will see a new star come down and rescue them. You'll get to play the fairy godmother, this time."

"And then what?"

"And then we go home, Centurion," *Lady Blackbeard* snapped. "Phil would have already gone that way, except that we were able to rescue *Persephone*, and then *Forgotten Mercy*. Those were all rolls of the dice, and this one will be even more so, but we've got the pieces in place this time. We've borrowed *Queen Anne's Revenge*, stolen *Packmule*, recovered *Persephone*, and now we have *Forgotten Mercy*. That's a pretty good outcome for a year on a lost frontier."

"It's just that…" she heard his voice trail off.

"What will you do when it's time?" she filled in.

Rather than speak, he nodded, but she could see the words, the terror in his eyes.

"It has been nearly eight years," he whispered in apparent agony.

"Is this the same crazy bastard that captured a hospital ship all by himself?" she asked, her voice growing coarse and sharp. "Walked in there with one barely-promoted-from-Landsman Spacer and made the entire crew afraid of you? Is this the same Granville Veitengruber?"

He nodded, still a little white around the edges, but perhaps breathing again.

"Then you're overthinking this," she said firmly. "You'll come in hard and fast and launch a whole, freaking phalanx of surprise death on those bastards, firing every gun you have. Just like First Expeditionary does it. Then you land and start organizing folks on the ground for rescue, as soon as the rest of us can get there."

"There are still other stations in orbit," Granville said.

"And we're outside of beam range," Siobhan countered, pounding on the man. "That leaves missiles, and *CS-405* is an escort specifically designed for that sort of thing. Plus, if they piss us off, I've heard Markus and Galin talking about heading over to *Mansi-D*."

"What in the world would they find there?" he asked, confused.

Good, she had gotten him off the ledge of his fear. Engaged his professional curiosity. Reminded him he was an officer.

"As I understand it from those two crazy rednecks, they want to rebuild one of the D-class hulls," Siobhan said. "Not the honeytrap, but one of the other ones. Then fly out somewhere and capture an asteroid, sail in and let it go on a ballistic arc that intersects with a station, but not the planet below."

"That's even more insane," his face grew confused.

"We've done it before," she said, watching his eyes grow huge with surprise. "Well, not us specifically, but the original group of Keller's folks: *Auberon*, *Rajput*, and *CR-264*. A decade ago, they did it against a group of pirates that had holed up on a moon somewhere. She told them to surrender, and then threw a rock at them. Gave them exactly that long to escape, and then everybody watched it impact and destroy the base."

"But how?" he asked her, still floating out there in some ethereal place.

"The physics is easy, Granvie," she said with a hungry smile. "You just have to be angry enough to actually want to do something like that to somebody. These are your people, sure. But they're also ours. Never forget that."

"I had," he admitted, after a long beat to process that tidbit. "I spent too long alone on *Abakn*, even after I found Deni. Forgotten what it was like to belong. To make a difference."

"We're here because of you, Veitengruber," she said. "And you will lead us into that final battle."

"Yes," he replied, finally meeting her eyes, with a firm conviction taking root in his. "I will."

ADMIRAL OF THE FLEET (FEBRUARY 10, 403)

BECAUSE IT WAS GOING to be that kind of day, Phil dug out his dress uniform from the air-tight bag in the back of the closet and had it pressed. Something about it just put his mind in the right place for this mission as he looked at his reflection in the mirror of his cabin.

He was only a lowly Command Centurion, in charge of Keller's smallest and least dangerous ship, but that hadn't stopped him from accidentally turning into the Acting Fleet Centurion for this task force of dangerous pirates he had assembled.

It had been ten months, lost at sea. Hopefully, in that time, Keller had been able to move the base someplace safe and get the rest of the ships rebuilt to come ravage *Buran* and maybe succeed.

He looked forward to standing at his Court Martial, when he got back, listing off all the decisions that he had made instead of simply coming home, and pointing to all the hell he and his folks had been able to raise in the *Altai* sector, and even reaching in to threaten the *Lena* sector enough to make them flinch. First Lord Naoumov hadn't been able to put him in a cruiser, but Phil sure as hell had proved that you didn't need one to do your job.

Keller had demanded crazy and violent as a way to get the common citizens of *The Holding* to fear their overlord less than they feared her. He had met enough of those people this year to understand that most of them were just folks. Trying to get by and make a living. Attempting to live a good life and have a little fun along the way.

It was only their God that needed to be overthrown. The rest of the civilization wasn't all that bad a place, once you got past that. Completely insane, but the citizens probably weren't any weirder than his own extended family back home. Possibly even less so, but every family was crazy in its own way.

He checked the time and pulled his tunic down one last time. He had lost weight over the year since he last had reason to wear this uniform. It hung a little baggy in places where it had been tight before.

Phil put that down to stress, more than anything, because they had eaten probably better over the last year than he would have had they remained in the harness with Keller.

One deep breath to center himself, and he emerged into the hallway.

It was only a few steps to the bridge, and only a few more to the primary conference room. That pirate, Bedrov, had done all the little things right, at least when designing his corvettes. There were cabins close to all the primary workspaces, like the bridge, engineering, and emergency bridge, rather than all clustered in one space where someone might have to run the length of the ship in an alert.

He was last to enter, but that was by design. His job today was to make an entrance. Everybody would already be there, including the Chief Medical Officer off *Forgotten Mercy*.

Dr. Sam Au wasn't one of his people. Wouldn't remain behind when it was all done and stay in the Empire, as he suspected a few might consider, especially if they found what he expected at *Mansi*.

Au hadn't even expressed anything more than sympathy with their cause, but Andre Gave had spoken up for having her here. The Dragoon had echoed the sentiment, and the two of them had spent the most time with the woman over the last month. Good enough for Phil.

They were seated as a trio at one corner of the conference table when he entered. Au went to rise, but fell back into her seat when she realized that nobody else had done more than look up.

She blushed and they shared a quick smile. Maybe her heart *was* in the right place. Her assistance in this endeavor would make it much more likely to succeed. Her resistance would just be friction to overcome.

Evan was at one end of the table, where he could gesture madly when it came time for the projection of *Mansi*, but most of these folks already knew what it looked like.

And what their jobs would be.

Lady Blackbeard and *Ground Control* were across from

the medical team, with Veitengruber beyond Heather. Bok was here, finally back in uniform for one last charge before he retired for good. Kam was across from Bok, providing a balance there, as well.

Phil had heard the stories of Able-Spacer Avelina Indovina and her plans to get herself made the Duke of *Lighthouse Station*. Bok apparently looked to retire there and possibly homestead the southern half of the lake. Or something.

We all have different happy places.

Phil walked to the end of the table, between Veitengruber and Andre, but remained standing just long enough to fix this image in his head. They would never again be together like this, he expected. Hell, given the last year, he could see First Lord breaking up this entire crew and sending them off to other vessels as a way of reintegrating some and promoting others, although it might also just infect other crews with the same craziness. That might not be a bad thing. Heather, Siobhan, and Evan were all due some sort of advancement for their work, and he probably was, as well.

Someone else would likely take command of *CS-405*.

And her legend.

Good luck living up to that, bucko.

He smiled. They smiled back, like his thoughts were in a bubble over his head. Maybe they were. You didn't build a team like this without being able to communicate non-verbally.

Phil pulled out the chair and sat.

"Doctor Au, thank you for joining us," he said formally to the woman. "This is not a planning session, per se, but perhaps one last drink among friends before battle."

"I see," she replied quietly.

Phil had spent a little time around Keller's tame defector, the old Khan of *Trusski*. Scholars of *The Holding* held themselves separate from the rest of society, above the Technicians, the Warriors, and the Artisans, as philosopher/kings from Plato's old model.

He didn't think it would work, but probably having a deathless God in your face all the time with the power to punish would keep the human tendency towards greediness and sloth in check.

"We are going to *Mansi*," Phil announced in a voice that left nobody surprised. "*Persephone* will be our Trojan Horse. If all goes as planned, we will eliminate the command station orbiting the planet, and then see if the other seven wish to surrender, or be destroyed in turn. Kam, I've read the notes from Tuason and Dunklin. If it comes to that, I think they'd be better off launching a whole bunch of smaller rocks at once, rather than a big one."

"Why?" Kam perked up. "One big one will be harder to kill."

"Actually, it would be easier to blast with the big guns until it broke apart," Bok spoke up gruffly. "Each shot deflects part of the rubble off course. Buckshot will require every individual rock be blasted. We forget who our target is."

Kam just fixed the Boatswain with an arched eyebrow, so Phil let them quibble.

"They don't have shields, Kam," Bok said. "Those

deflect rocks, too. Those stations have power absorbers. Great against explosions and beams. Worthless against a ton or six of nickel-iron moving at high speed."

"Exactly," Phil agreed. "But I hope we won't have to go there. Or if we do, that it's only one, until everyone comes around."

"How do we round them up afterwards?" Trinidad asked. "Boarding parties?"

"Negative," Phil said. "I'll order them to abandon ship in lifepods. Then we'll spike the empty stations with guns. They can live on the ground for a while, until someone comes along to rescue them. It was good for the goose."

"Then we come into play?" Andre asked, turning to include Dr. Au in his question.

"Yes," Phil agreed. "*Packmule* and *Forgotten Mercy* will stay out at the edge of the system, ready to run if something goes wrong. Once military operations cease, I'll need you both down in orbit. We'll gather up as many men as we can, as well as supplies from the surface, and then sail straight home to *Osynth B'Udan*. If we can't get everyone on the first pass, we'll come back with a second fleet for the rest. If we can, then we're home and we can send all our prisoners back to their own lives. That includes your medical staff, Dr. Au."

"I still find it hard to believe that we would not become permanent prisoners ourselves, Director Kosnett," she replied evenly, if a touch quieter.

Her voice had all the emotional loading removed, but he could still see the fear in her eyes. After all, it might be good for the gander, as well.

"I will not allow it," Phil said simply, in as grim a voice

as he had.

Veitengruber pounded a fist on the table, while others echoed the sentiment.

"I do not understand," Dr. Au complained.

Phil started to speak, but Heather leaned in and got his attention, obviously wanting to say something. He nodded and leaned back.

"We met a defector from *The Holding*, Dr. Au," Ground Control said. "He explained that, as he saw things, the purpose of your civilization was to provide the highest possible level of ethical interaction between people. That *The Holding* would eventually absorb the entire galaxy, by providing the best example of a proper life."

"Well yes, of course," the other woman agreed. "All Scholars are taught that, and in turn teach it to other castes."

"The defector had come to *Fribourg* to try to reach Imperial Scholars, Dr. Au," Heather's voice turned a shade darker now as Phil listened, keeping his own scowl hidden. "After *The Eldest* attempted to destroy *St. Legier*, he defected and renounced his name and birthright, because he saw that attempt as the greatest possible failing of *Buran* and everything it stood for. It was no longer: *Join us and see how much better your lives can be*, Doctor. *The Eldest* had drawn it in much starker terms: *Submit, or I will destroy you*. You have ceded the moral and ethical high ground, and will never recover it."

Phil found Au's blush fascinating. Obviously, the woman wanted to argue. To negate everything Heather had just said.

And could not. *All* ethical arguments fail when you are reduced to orbital bombardments of innocent civilians to make your point.

She subsided instead, slamming her mouth shut and obviously grinding her teeth from the way her jaw muscles moved.

But at the end of the day, there just wasn't much you could say to any of that.

"So while we understand that many of you have high ethical standards, Dr. Au," Phil concluded the thought, "many of us believe that you are in service to evil. *Fribourg* and *Aquitaine* did not and will not keep slaves. They both captured prisoners and sent them home. They did not trade all that much directly, but allowed neutral nations to operate without significant hassle. Humans were given as much freedom as they could handle, rather than answering to a God in real time. Because we will all have to explain ourselves to the Creator, one of these days."

The room fell silent. Sam Au took a deep breath and released it, eyes still focused on the tabletop in front of her, rather than any of the people.

Finally she looked up at him. Phil could see much of the same pain in the back of her eyes that Seeker had brought with him from *St. Legier*.

Who likes to wake up and suddenly question everything in a new light?

"Was all of this for my benefit?" she asked, gesturing to the room.

"Only some, Doctor," Phil replied evenly. "The rest was to impress upon you that we are doing all of this for our own higher motives. And that everyone in this room will fight anybody that decides not to send you home when it is all done.”

“Including Keller?” she asked. “I have seen and heard the reports of her swath of destruction across *Altai*.”

“I honestly believe that we could replace everyone in this room with the crew off of any other vessel in First Expeditionary Fleet, and the conversation would not have changed that much,” Phil said. “Keller has ordered retaliation for *St. Legier*, but she does so because she wanted the people of *The Holding* to understand what *The Eldest* did. Her war is with the God, the *Buran* itself, and the Warriors who bomb innocent worlds from orbit. You are not a Warrior, so you are not my enemy.”

The blush was back. Phil suspected the woman was having a massive crisis of conscience today, which actually had been his plan, not that he had told anyone else. The surge of blood into the face just meant that her emotions were too close to the surface.

Keller had demanded that the people of *The Holding* fear her more than they did *Buran* itself, so that they would not do anything significant to prevent her intended *deicide*.

And Phil really wanted to be there when that woman killed a God.

“I cannot speak for my crew,” Au said in a tiny voice, still not angry or afraid. “But I believe I understand now. And we will try.”

“That’s all anyone can do, Dr. Au,” Phil answered her. “Find the ethical solution. We must seek to make the galaxy a better place than we found it.”

From deep space, the system was peaceful. Almost placid, as Granville watched the sensor feed come in from Evan Brinich aboard *CS-405*.

One yellow-orange semi-dwarf of about one and a half solar masses. Six major planets in orbit, with *B* in the habitable zone and *D* out further, with a junkyard of lost dreams on the surface of one of her moons. Eight stations on a cubical, defensive orbit above the main planet, capable of covering every centimeter of approach, but not providing any significant overlap of firepower.

Why should they? Who would be crazy enough to try something like this?

Out at the edge of the system, nothing had changed since he had last watched this system dance.

A light flickered on, on the console in front of him.

"Veitengruber," he said, opening the channel to the flagship.

The lifesuit he was wearing today included heavy

gloves, so simple tasks were a little harder. But it also took him back to flying a Starfighter, when he had that same weight on his movements. As opposed to facing space with nothing around him.

"Kosnett," the Admiral replied. "Stand by to make your first Jump. We will enter JumpSpace in thirty seconds."

"Understood, sir," Granville said, nodding unconsciously as he did.

They were doing it the Imperial way, today. He laughed to himself before opening the intercom so he could talk to everyone.

In *Aquitaine*, the Command Centurion turned over fighting to the Tactical Officer, so they could watch the rest of the ship. Normally, Heather or Siobhan would have handled that task, but *Ground Control* and *Lady Blackbeard* were each aboard their own ships today. Evan Brinich would have normally taken over for them, and was pretty good at it from what Granville understood from the others, but Phil needed him in command of the massive sensor arrays on the scout.

Today, those installations were going to be most of *CS-405*'s firepower, so Phil would revert to being his own Tactical Officer, like a good Imperial Captain, just as Granville had aboard *Persephone*.

Needs must, when the devil drives.

"All hands, stand by for JumpSpace," Granville said in as calm and commanding a voice as he could manage, at a time when his voice still wanted to crack and his hands shake.

He had pasted a small, printed image of Deni on his

console. He reached out and touched it once, missing his love.

Granville watched the flagship vanish, leaving him with the other vessels, but only for a few seconds. *CS-405* was using the equivalent of human-calculated JumpDrives, so they were slower and a little less accurate than *Persephone*'s JumpSails. And the others were staying up here for a day or so, until they got the signal from the Admiral that everything was fine for them to join him down in the sunshine.

Hopefully, Granville would still be alive tomorrow to greet them. That was not a given, considering today's task. But Deni would survive, even if he didn't. The Admiral had offered to officiate a wedding, but neither man had been able to take that step yet. Perhaps they would both be able to face it after this battle.

NovLao as a culture was less concerned about such things as two men in love, but Deni had been raised in a very traditional, church-inflected family. He was almost as lost at this point as a young man raised to the martial glories of Imperial service, in a land where homosexuals were at best ridiculed, and at worst murdered by their own families.

"Transitioning to JumpSpace," Granville said.

His voice might have cracked, but he could always blame the excitement of being back in service and about to enter battle, if asked.

As lies went, it was a reasonably believable one.

Granville focused on the projected course that would rendezvous with *CS-405* shortly, before he began that thing that his history lessons kept wanting to call the *Charge of the Light Brigade.*

Onward, forward, into the valley of death.

He only rode with five companions today, so perhaps Childe Roland, sounding his horn instead. Hopefully, his would be a happier legend in the retelling.

RealSpace.

On a Jump this short, avoiding the orbital plane in order to come in low, the flight had taken little time. Only the gravity of the star and the density of the solar wind were significant impacts on navigation.

Twenty light-minutes from *Mansi-B.* Passive sensors only. Dead stop relative to all motion. Wait.

Ninety seconds later, a ping. Laser comm had established a lock and received a burst transmission.

CS-405 had found him.

"*Persephone*, this is Kosnett," the burst message read. "We have you locked. *CS-405* is at battle stations and ready. You have the flag. *Godspeed.*"

Granville took a moment to wipe his eyes and sniff back tears at the sudden emotions that threatened to overwhelm him. He toggled the transponders on, because any ship coming out of Jump that close and that fast was automatically an enemy vessel, and he wanted those bastards to know who had come for them.

IFV Persephone. Seventeenth Imperial Police Protectorate.

Your doom.

Not Roland after all, as he thought about it.

George.

"All hands, this is Granville Veitengruber," he said into

the intercom and the logs. And history. "I have the flag. Accelerating to attack speed. Prepare for battle."

One button on his console controlled the shields, pitiful as they were on a police cutter. They were a matter of exclamation point, rather than defense, because station batteries would go through them like wet tissue paper.

Still, Granville was a warrior, and he needed his shield when facing a dragon.

The second button unlocked the three guns, a single Type-3 on the bow and defensive Type-1's on the flanks.

When facing a dragon, he needed a sword.

Finally, the engines, accelerating on a smooth curve as he brought them more and more on-line, trusting that Bardeen was monitoring them and would get him where he needed to be.

The knight is nothing without his steed, charging proudly into battle. Even against a fire-breathing dragon.

Granville watched the gauges as the charge built, thunder rumbling heavily across the field in his mind as the entire weight of the Imperial Fleet gathered speed behind him. They would be coming out of this Jump at the highest speed that Heather had been able to calculate would let him insert into the atmosphere cleanly, instead of bouncing somewhere off the thickening air and surfacing too close to another station with a long rifle.

Finally, the targeting console on his left. Hard-wired onto a second stand welded in place by Galin Tuason, the last of *Persephone*'s three plankholders, to give them sixteen missiles in tubes around the outside of his hull.

Because when facing the dragon, St. George needed his lance.

Granville took a deep breath.

"Now," he said simply, trusting that everyone listening would understand. He wasn't sure his voice could say anything more.

Persephone leapt into JumpSpace.

THE DRAGON (FEBRUARY 17, 403)

ON HIS SCREENS, Granville knew exactly where the primary command station for the *Mansi* system was located. All orders and traffic had originated from it, and very little had gone out from other stations, except in response.

And he knew exactly where the normal edge of the gravity well for *Mansi-B* was located. All ships with JumpSails had nifty sensors built-in to conservatively locate that place where you should stop. The high-tide mark, as it were.

Going any deeper risked overloading the fragile matrix that made JumpSails work in the first place. Then you had to zero everything and realign all the bits and pieces until the ship could fly safely again.

Siobhan had explained Alber' d'Maine to him. *The Berserker*. Others had gone a step further and let him read a concise report about Tomas Kigali's epic flight from *Ladaux* to *Ballard*, racing against an Imperial fleet set to destroy *Alexandria Station* and the library contained therein.

CR-264 had done this exact same thing then, riding the system past the point where the ship wanted to drop into RealSpace, until he was forced out as the energy gradients climbed higher than the matrix could hold. In Kigali's instance, he had been trying to set a new record, point to point, and had come very close to the mathematical minimum-time-sail possible between the two worlds.

In the aftermath, *CR-264* had simply come out of Jump as close as possible, and then executed a double-slingshot around the planet before the ship was able to slow down enough to drop into orbit.

Persephone was going to top that today. Granville and his crew were going to come out as deep as possible into the gravity well, and open fire as soon as they could achieve lock, before diving headlong into the atmosphere and try to slow down enough to land safely without flying into range of one of the other stations.

All the while expecting everybody out there to launch missiles at him. Because the others were likely to be a touch angry, after his surprise.

The survivors, anyway.

Persephone's engines and sails were old. Tuned by hand in the middle of a cattle ranch, rather than in a proper orbital dry-dock. Good enough for the task at hand, but nowhere near enough to be smooth.

The ship emerged into RealSpace with a lurch so hard that Granville thought they had slammed into orbital traffic, such as a cubesat or something small. No loss of atmosphere, so hopefully all was good. Everyone was in their suits, because of that risk, but he had to be prepared.

Bad things were going to happen. He just wanted them to happen to the other guys instead.

Or at least first.

The sensors came back with a hard lock almost immediately, as close as they were when they emerged. The station was almost exactly below him, a hollow hexagon design, aligned with the planetary surface.

It was like looking into an open, gray eye to see the blue and white clouds beneath.

Or an arrow falling out of the sky at a bullseye.

"Engage," Granville ordered, just in case anybody wasn't going to fire as soon as they could hit something. The Type-1 beams were a little beyond the edge of effective range, but that was going to change shortly.

Already, the hull whispered under the pressure of air, even as tenuous as it was this high in the sky.

Granville confirmed all sixteen missiles showed green lights and pounded his fist into the big, green button in the middle of the screen, marked *Havoc*. He didn't get the joke, but others had apparently gotten hooked on some ancient writer.

And these certainly qualified as *Dogs of War*, to quote Galin and Markus.

Leomiti's bow gun fired, lashing out at the station and slamming into the starboard edge of the ring, as seen from directly overhead. Granville didn't have time to look at the sensors and see if the shot had been stopped by a panel, or lightly deflected, or even just slammed into bare metal. The logs would show it tomorrow, if anybody cared.

On the screen in front of him, the world turned white.

For the briefest second, Granville thought something had burned out somewhere, a stress overload or a circuit failure killing all his cameras, but then *Persephone* blasted through the exhaust of sixteen missiles all launching within a second of each other.

It was like a modern art exhibit, staring down a corridor made of giant icicles, until you realized that each of those was a harpoon racing madly to kill a whale.

Airspeed indications had slowed, almost exactly to the degree Heather had predicted. *Persephone* was still falling, a meteor racing towards the ground, but he could nose in now, once they got low enough, and then hopefully pull a wide, orbiting spiral down until the engines could hold them.

Anything, rather than have to broach to one side and take fire from somebody else.

Spier's gun fired next. Granville had no idea what her target was, or even if she hit the station. He was focused on flying right now, trying to keep the ship centered so both flank guns could do something. If the defenders were on the ball, they might be able to fire a missile back right now, when he had no maneuverability and a closure rate so high that it would be there before anybody could react.

The fog of falling arrows in front of him didn't help his peace of mind, so he toggled to a targeting radar instead. That just showed the ass end of his missiles and the ring of the station coming towards him at a speed that kept screaming *Impact Imminent* in his subconscious.

A light flashed out, so close that he thought *Persephone* had flown into a sunbeam accidentally from some lunar shadow. A moment later, his brain processed that as an inbound beam that had missed. He had no idea what they were shooting at, either, and didn't care right now.

Time to make this Kigali fellow look junior varsity. After all, the man had been doing his antics in a cutter like this one. But Granville Veitengruber had cut his teeth in an A-6j melee fighter. His were the crazy people.

"All hands, hang on to something stable," he yelled.

In a situation like this, everybody should already be seated and belted in. But the grav-plates were likely going to be the first thing to fail, if the guns needed power.

And he was about to get outrageously stupid.

Javelins fall with a wobble inherit in any muscle-powered missile. Arrows do the same.

Bullets spiral, having come out of a rifled barrel under high pressure that translated into speed and friction.

Mansi-B was laid out below him like a map, with a ring marking buried treasure almost exactly in the center. Granville pushed the ship into a side loop.

Pitch is the description of the bow going up and down, relative to the attitude of flight. Yaw is the side-to-side motion. Roll turns in place like an alligator with a still-kicking antelope in its teeth. And then you added more motion to carve out a giant circle.

Up, over, and across in a clockwise spiral, as seen from someone trailing him with a camera as he twisted onto his starboard wing.

Another flash of light. Again, more an elusive memory than an experience, but it might have intersected with one of the missiles inbound on that station. No time to consider. No place to remain.

Persephone rolled again under his touch, this time to port with a flare of side-slip thrown in as he skittered the nose out and up a shade in the middle of the grander motion.

Most ships would maintain the cycle when rolling like this. That was predictable, since jerking the hull back and forth stressed internal frames and aged your spacecraft at a hideous pace.

Someone down there had been expecting another starboard roll. A shot went by like lightning striking a nearby tree. All of the heavens were aglow, and Granville thought he could see an ionization trail reaching back to the station.

Big guns. And they missed.

Ten seconds to flyby. Three seconds to impact. Granville pushed the bow down and held pitch while spiraling madly in place like an ice skater pulling their arms in for speed. The crew would begin losing the contents of their stomachs if he held this too long, so he let go of the roll and flattened himself back into a clean dive.

The bow of *Persephone* wasn't centered on the station any more. He would fly by them at the mark of eight o'clock.

All the hordes of hell appeared to open portals and vomit forth at the same time. White skies underneath him turned red and orange as missiles got home. He couldn't tell what the effect had been without more time than he had, because right now, the risk was slamming into the orbital debris he had created.

Hopefully, the station was mortally wounded and

about to fall out of the sky in great, messy pieces that he would miss, because there was no way in hell to maneuver now.

Secondary explosions? Or late missiles? No way to tell.

Something big went boom again with a flash more than a second after the big firestorm. Granville lined up the station overhead and dove away from it as well as he could, careful not to turn turtle and start to tumble.

It was one thing to do this in snubfighter. It was something else again in a police cutter.

All three guns fired again, almost simultaneously. He could only tell because they overloaded the circuits and the grav-plates cut out until Isiah could reset things. The bridge lights went dark at the same time, but the screens were still on, so the ship hadn't died.

And then something crunched and all the consoles went black.

THE CAVALRY (FEBRUARY 17, 403)

AND AFTER ALL THAT, Phil ended up in Tactical Command again. After all his arguments with himself about being graceful in letting Heather handle the task without any advice from him, when she was so good at. How he needed to be in charge and act like a Command Centurion.

Heather wasn't here. Siobhan was absent, as well. Normally, Evan would have graduated to Tactical now. He was coming along, but right now, Phil needed the man's genius on the sensors today, jamming the living shit out of that station and her gunners. Anything less and they might not pull this off.

So Command Centurion Philip Kosnett, being his own Tactical Officer, just like Heather, Siobhan, and Granville Veitengruber were doing as well, this squadron stretched as far and as thin as the crew could hold.

"All hands, stand by for combat," Phil said aloud,

letting the comm system pick it up and route it out to all decks.

Yeoman West Lovisone was flying the ship today, something of a thesis defense in a very unforgiving school of hard knocks. He glanced up now and nodded at Phil over his console, eyes maybe a little more squinted than usual and fingers probably stiff with tension.

Unlike *Persephone*, *CS-405* would be coming out at a time when the station was alert. And they would be coming in relatively slowly, compared to the insane speeds Heather had calculated to bring Veitengruber to safety. Assuming nothing failed.

Thus, he needed Evan. Needed both sensor arrays hosing the station down with all the electronic countermeasures and noise that the ship could generate, like spotlights blinding ancient pilots attempting to find a target to bomb.

"Gun crews, you are unlocked," Phil said ominously. They were still in JumpSpace. Normally that command didn't happen until they had emerged and had a target. Right now, *Persephone* was the only thing out there NOT to shoot at. "Engage as you bear."

No need to give them orders about shooting priorities. If it wasn't Veitengruber and it was moving, it needed to die as fast as someone could lay a targeting reticle on it. If nothing appeared, put all fire into the station until either died or surrendered.

Emergence.

The ship was coming out hot, but had to stay maneuverable. They were above the high-water mark of the gravity well, so they should be able to dodge back out if they had to, something else *Persephone* couldn't do with their mad dash in.

Evan had the station on the screen. Like the gun crews, he had the responsibility to protect the ship.

"Locked and engaged," the Science Officer called without looking up.

The Tactical Officer needed to know that the bad guys were going to have a hard time finding them.

"Pilot, take her in," Phil ordered, watching his screens. "All ahead cruising speed, stay atop the station and keep the ring centered until we get close."

"Aye, sir," the pilot replied.

Unlike Heather, Phil had always let his pilots handle the fine tuning. Aim them at a target, but let them dial in the nose and the speed, rather than providing exact angles. Here, something like that would make West stop and think at a time when every moment was critical. Let him fly things. Phil hadn't forgotten ship handling when he added his third stripe.

They were just about perfect with their timing as they came out of Jump. The station below them was utterly wreathed in fire as *405*'s bow came into line and surged ahead. Evan added a circle on the screen to indicate where his sensors picked up the cutter, just about to pass the fireball the man had unleashed.

Phil shifted all extra power forward into the bow shields.

"Turret Boren, engage the station now," Phil ordered.

They were outside of effective range, and everybody knew it, but right now, he wanted to start tapping on their shoulder over there. Veitengruber was in close and had stirred up a hornet nest. But he couldn't survive long in this atmosphere.

CS-405 needed to come to his rescue. And they had the shielding to handle some level of incoming fire.

"West, start a port roll," Phil said. "Keep me zeroed, but I want to spin on the hook if that bastard has anything left."

The screen wanted to lock the target on the station, but Phil overrode and let it rotate on his screen, so he had an actual feel of the situation below him.

"Turret Chester and Wiley, hold for defense," Phil continued, keeping the two innermost turrets passive for now. That bastard had missiles, if he remembered how to use them with all the crap going wrong right now. "Turret Yalu, engage as you bear."

Why the hell not? West was going to be shifting the bow around as he maneuvered. It was possible that the stern would come around enough for a deflection shot. Plus, once Phil turned his back on the station, if it still existed, that crew would need to be locked in anyway. Might as well start them on it now.

"Evan, get me a damage report of the station," Phil said, probably louder than he needed to, but that was the adrenaline and mad energy in his system. "And find Veitengruber, too."

Long enough pause that Phil took a breath and stepped back in his head.

Act like an Admiral, too. Remember that. You've got a squadron that needed to be commanded, not just a deck here.

"Station has suffered severely, Tactical," Evan said.

"Several sections appear to be off-line, but others are trying to lock weapons on us. We're negotiating now."

Phil laughed, imagining a hectoring *Buran* weapons tech trying to do something while Evan slapped him about the head with a tree branch. Silly, but the sound of the voice was just there.

"Where's *Persephone*?" Phil asked.

"I think she's been hit, sir," Evan said. "Hard to tell, but she's not maneuvering like she should, and all outbound fire has ceased."

"We need to buy Veitengruber time, then," Phil said. "West, accelerate in closer. We're going to have to beat those bastards to death here."

"Roger that, sir," West yelled. He was also too loud, but this was his first time flying something this big in a situation this messy.

Graduation day, Yeoman.

"Tactical, I am getting launch warnings from the four stations at our horizons," Evan said. "Inbound missiles, but we've got time, and they'll probably be ballistic by the time they get here."

Ballistic.

Phil chuckled to himself.

Launched at a set of coordinates and maybe a little terminal tracking capability, but certainly not capable of doing anything, with their fuel long since burned out. At least it would give Chester and Wiley something to do, if anybody guessed even remotely accurately.

Phil had no intention of staying around here. But every missile some range officer launched now was one less later on, when it might be important.

He could just see some base commander standing behind the weapons advocate, yelling at them to do something, anything. Even stupid things.

Boren hadn't let up on her fire, metronomically woodpeckering as the guns got closer and the focus got good enough to maybe hurt.

"Gun crews, I have launch warnings on our bow," Evan yelled.

Phil relaxed. He didn't need to speak.

Evan had given the alert they needed.

Chester cut loose now, even without a target through the expanding gas clouds. You might always get lucky and hit a warhead in the tube or just coming clear. It was a bad time for a missile to suddenly explode, since it was so close to others, and you had a bay door open for all that plasma to roll back into.

CS-405 was a Corvette/Scout. An escort who never got the fancy jobs or the glory when hanging out with bigger, meaner cousins. Chester's gun team might even have a little bit of a chip on their shoulders about that, and be in a position to maybe answer the critics today.

The hull crunched hard with a flash of light that filled the whole bridge. Station gun had finally found them. Wasn't a square hit, but ran down a flank. Like maybe the ship they were shooting at was dodging and spinning away from the gunners trying to hit it?

Gosh.

"Turret Boren, overload your gun," Phil ordered.

"Tactical, please confirm overload," a woman's voice answered a second later.

Boren's Gun Captain, asking if he was sure he wanted

to risk the gun blowing up right now, when they started firing faster than the cooling systems could keep up. It was frequently a recipe for disaster. And it would absolutely cause so much wear that they would have to replace the entire gun well ahead of the regular schedule.

Add that to the list of things at the Court Martial, First Lord. One of mine's down there without anybody but us to protect him.

"Boren, override confirmed," Phil said. "Go to rapid fire and damn the torpedoes."

Risk.

Balanced against need and reward. Maybe the gun would overheat and have to completely shut down in the middle of battle. Maybe something would explode, like had happened to the JumpMatrix generators and controls.

Shit happens, the cry of all commanders, to the anguish of their engineers.

Chester's fire had pulsed hard once, and then fallen into a regular pattern as missiles began to climb out of the gravity well at them. That was the hardest shot in the world to make for a missile gunner. The damned thing had to climb against gravity, appearing to sit perfectly still in the sky below as the gunners tracked it. Only *CS-405*'s roll would affect defensive fire, and even then they were staying in a tight enough circle to keep the shots well-centered.

Boren picked up their rate of fire, a mad writer pounding away at the keys as he approached to the end of Act Three.

Flash of light, crunch of damage. This one had been more square, rather than that first, almost-ranging shot.

Phil watched his shield readouts flicker. Dorsal had taken most of the first, with only a few places where energy had hit hull, and most of that insulated.

This one had been starboard side and nearly nose on. Which was actually a better result for Phil. All the extra energy forward in the shields had absorbed a lot of it, letting only leakage through again. It was like getting stabbed to death with an icepick, doing this, but those batteries were roughly equivalent to the Type-4's he would have faced back home. He could handle losing insulation and outer chambers when the blows got softened along the way.

"Secondary explosions on the station," Evan said aloud. "Chester got a missile in the tube. Two more incoming."

"Boren, shift to defensive fire now," Phil yelled.

He hadn't told them to stop the overload, so it was almost like watching a firehose shift down. But the further-out missile got caught in the fire, almost at the same moment that Chester caught the nearer one.

Lights began to dance on the station's hull as Phil watched. More beams hitting bare metal rather than splashing on power absorbers. Who in the hell…?

Ha. Yalu had a clear shot as the spin had gotten a little too wide, and tagged the station.

"Evan. Station status?" Phil asked.

"Wide-spread failures of the defensive array, Tactical," the man replied. "Something just broke over there."

"Pilot, ride the gyros now," Phil commanded in a voice that wouldn't brook argument. "Cut your drives and bring the bow about until you lay me a broadside. Boren, return to normal fire. All guns engage as you lie."

Assents up and down the scale as everyone checked in. Probably with a hint of maniacal laughter, with what was about to happen.

This was the best part of the new corvette designs. The old destroyers and light cruisers barely had enough gyros to walk and chew bubblegum at the same time. Heavy cruisers were a little better, but not much. Trying a bootlegger in anything but *CS-405* probably would have resulted in complete systems failures and street pizza across the entirety of orbit.

Fortunately, he had awesome engineers, and the craziest crew in the fleet.

CS-405 began to turn. Her engines had stopped pushing, but the bow was flaring, and the mass of the ship was rotating inside that, an arrow falling off the flight and beginning to tumble.

Except arrows can't fire at someone as they go.

Boren hadn't let up her mad fire, but slowed now. Chester was actually almost in a perfect reciprocal, snare drum and bass going back and forth. Yalu had kept lock and West had been smart enough or lucky enough to slew the bow out along the line that let the aft station keep firing.

And then Wiley got into the act.

Phil hadn't gotten to listen to all four Type-1-Pulse batteries light it up at once since that idiot Nightmaster had flown right through the middle of the squadron at *Trusski*. The symphony of destruction brought a smile to his face.

And time for ship-handling now.

"West, ahead slow only," Phil ordered. "Balance us out and push us just a little off line with the station. Then figure out how to keep the broadside on arc as we pass. All batteries, continue firing until the station comes apart or they surrender. Maintain your guns, though. We're not done here."

Four lights flickering green on his board. Possibly the equivalent of all four gun captains rolling their eyes at the man suggesting they didn't know how to kill things.

"Evan, how's *Persephone*?"

"Stand by, Tactical."

FREEFALL (FEBRUARY 17, 403)

SUDDENLY, he was back at *Samara*, and seven years hadn't passed. His fighter was dead in space and there was nothing he could do but watch an enemy destroyer close and wonder if it was going to destroy or capture him.

Except this was the present, not the past. Granville was aboard *Persephone*, and the planet below him was *Mansi-B*.

The ship was still dead to the controls.

"Isiah, I need power," he roared as loud as he could.

The internal radio in his suit would have transmitted a whisper right now, but Granville wasn't in that place in his mind.

At least he still had atmosphere around him. If they had suffered a square hit, all the air would have rushed out and left him with a poofed up suit and stiff joints. And a lot more panic as things fell silent around him with no air to reverberate.

So, somewhere aft, a shot had grazed something. It wasn't like he had shields capable of stopping whatever that bolt was. Hells, a Type-1 might have gone through those deflectors.

"Working," came the faint response. "Lost all aft arrays at the fuse."

Granville had no idea what that meant, except that his Systems Engineer seemed to understand how to fix it.

They were still in freefall right now, going towards the unforgiving surface of the planet at too high a rate. And accelerating.

From the feel of gravity around him, the bow of *Persephone* was pointed almost straight down right now. That made sense, with the narrow, smooth cylinder of the ship providing the least amount of resistance. There was still a small amount of roll going on as well, but softer than the one he had been attempting under fire. Not even enough to make him throw up. He couldn't speak for the rest of the crew.

A noise behind him sounded suspiciously like one of the flank guns.

"Who has power?" Granville said.

"Port gun," Spier replied. "And we're being chased by at least one missile right now. Engaging at max range."

"Bardeen?" Granville called.

"Surge overload, Commander," the engineer aft replied. "Isiah and I are trying to patch it."

There was nothing like sitting in a semi-dark bridge, lit by only the emergency lights, and counting the kilometers you were falling, utterly blind. Still, he was in command. Panicking wouldn't do anyone any good.

He reached out and touched Deni's picture once more, noting how little his hands seemed to shake.

More fire aft, plus a lot of cursing over the radio.

"Morgan, you should be live," Isiah's voice came over the line.

Sure enough, the hull began to ring in harmony as the starboard gun also engaged.

"Anyone?" Granville asked in a conversational voice.

"Getting close," Bardeen growled. "Figured guns first would be a good idea right now."

"Agreed, Arla," Granville said. "Just wondering."

"Working my ass off, top," came the reply.

He let that one alone. They were. This crew had been trusted by Admiral Kosnett to do the single most difficult job imaginable, and do it well.

Based on the size of the explosion before he lost all his aft cameras, they might have even succeeded. Now they just had to avoid slamming into the ground at orbital speeds, if they could.

The mission was already a success if the station was gone. Kosnett and his people could rescue everyone below.

It would have been nice to be there to say hello to the people he was about to rescue, though. And hold Deni one last time.

"Got you, you bastard," Spier snarled over the radio.

Must have. Fire ceased. Hopefully for lack of targets and not failure of whatever systems his engineers were trying to fix.

Lights came back on.

His console lit up and rebooted.

Gravity suddenly began to change its mind about down.

"Bridge, did that work?" Isiah called.

"Affirmative," Granville said. "I have power now. Positive control in twenty seconds."

"Roger that, bridge," Isiah replied. "Everyone stay suited. We've had to reroute life support out of the mix until we can take something apart and pull out whatever piece cooked when the system arced. Maybe a fix on the ground, or we can ask Kam for help."

"Understood," Granville said, typing his password furiously into the screen. Then slowing down and typing it correctly the second time.

The control screens came up and warned him that the ship was currently inside an atmosphere and in freefall. Did he wish to activate the engines?

Granville suppressed the phrase that he wanted to answer with. The judges at his eventual Court Martial might insist on ordering his mouth washed out with soap.

One tap, and thrusters found aft.

Spin settled as he let the autopilot nag him about unsafe maneuvering.

Sensors came live. Communications lit up with a whole bunch of scrambled transmissions, plus a few where people had apparently forgotten they were on a clear channel.

"*Persephone*, this is *CS-405*, answer please," Evan Brinich's voice came suddenly through the ether. Granville wasn't sure anything had ever been more wonderful.

"*Persephone*," Granville said. "Recovering from total power failure now. Not sure our status. Give me sixty seconds."

"Roger that," Evan said. "Standing by."

Gravity had a solid, if queasy hold now, tugging his

butt into his chair even as he wanted to keep falling forward into the bow of the ship.

"All hands, stand by for maneuvering," Granville said. His voice even sounded unremarkable, which was the remarkable part.

Now the fun part.

The ground was two thousand kilometers below him, and he was approaching it at four thousand kilometers per hour. And accelerating. Heather had calculated a flight path that involved spiraling down across a cylinder several hundred kilometers across, but he was supposed to have started that about ten minutes ago.

He engaged it anyway, and then overrode the polite parameters she had put in and let the tail of *Persephone* drop down further than it wanted.

"About to light the engines hard. Everyone strap in tight," Granville said.

He counted to ten and pressed a button, watching the fuel feeds slowly increase with burn, until the force of gravity seemed to be the back of the ship. He went ahead and cut the grav-plates out of the mix, just to keep people from having three possible downs as they got lower.

Outside hull temperature was well above normal, and climbing. And why the hell not? At least he wasn't trying to bleed off speed with friction by gliding, although they had been doing that before.

Harder thrust now. Down became aft as *Persephone* stood on her ass and the engines tried to push her back into space. Wouldn't, but the predicted elevation at which the ship reached zero vertical velocity stopped being kilometers underground, which was good.

The air was thicker now. Better media for the engines to push against. He could feel the increased bite. He eased off the throttle as the velocity of the fall approached zero, passing into a slight climb instead of the galaxy's biggest and worst Immelmann maneuver, the hammerhead stall.

He pushed *Persephone*'s nose over and suddenly down felt right. Gravity even lined up with the horizon of the deck.

"*Persephone*, this is *CS-405*," Evan broke his silence. "Missile launch signals detected, transmitting flight coordinates now. Looks like someone wants to try to shoot you down. Be advised when landing."

"Roger that," Granville said, opening the accompanying file.

"Bring it," Spier growled over the common line.

Someone else laughed. Probably Bardeen, from the tone.

Huh. Sure enough, someone actually launched missiles into an atmosphere. Against a moving target with sensors on. It was almost an impossible shot, but he could see them perhaps trying to catch him on the ground later. It was likely that at least one or two stations would be able to either see him or guess where he was close enough to launch something and let it guide itself when it was low enough.

Still, he had maneuverability and guns. And two gunners with a point to prove, from the grumbling back there.

Granville opened the map and looked for the kremlin defending the landing zone. Kosnett and Brinich would keep anyone from getting above him. He had the interesting job, now.

There.

Almost in the middle of a large prairie, on the south bank of a relatively large river. From thirty thousand meters, it looked almost idyllic, but Kosnett had assumed some level of orbital defenses on the ground, just exactly in case someone snuck close.

Rather than find out, he banked away and went to full power on the engines. It had been all of seventeen minutes since he had come out of Jump and lit the station on fire.

If *CS-405* was still overhead, he had succeeded.

By now the folks on the ground were probably awake, too.

OVERWATCH (FEBRUARY 17, 403)

"*Persephone*, this is *CS-405*," Phil heard Evan say. "Missile launch signals detected, transmitting flight coordinates now. Looks like someone wants to try to shoot you down. Be advised when landing."

Phil double-checked his boards. Eleven missiles had been launched at him from orbital stations earlier. Five more were currently joining them, but aimed down rather than across. Tricky shot from here, but not impossible.

He bracketed one of the stations on his screen and sent the note to both Evan and West.

"Let's get closer to this guy," Phil ordered. "He seems to be the most interested in doing something, having fired the most missiles. Take me deeper into the atmosphere so we can try to pick off the two he just sent after Granville. Plus get the four arcing across the sky above us."

"Yes, sir," the pilot chirped.

West seemed to have settled himself well. You never knew until people had been through the fire, what kind of individual would emerge, but Weston Lovisone had passed with flying colors.

Even the crazy stuff, like executing a skid on the gyros at the edge of the atmosphere.

Phil called up the view from a rear camera, currently centered and tracking on the remains of the station. One of those secondary explosions had turned into tertiaries. All weapons fire had ceased like a light switch had been thrown. Power absorber panels had failed, unleashing a whole other rime of explosions and destruction to top what Granville had unleashed.

They were picking up lifepods now, as folks decided maybe they wanted to be safe on the ground, rather than dead in low orbit.

"Gun captains," Phil called out. "Six targets identified on two paths. Kill them."

He cut the channel and went back to his boards. Moving this direction, two of the stations vanished beneath the horizon, and there did not appear to be anything but tiny communication relay satellites up here. Certainly nothing to guide them if they wanted to keep firing missiles.

He couldn't get close enough to any other station to do anything constructive. Or destructive, for that matter, but if this fool kept launching missiles, Phil was tempted to let Galin and the engineers kill him with rocks before anybody else was ordered to surrender.

Outbound fire as the various guns began to track and zero down for kills. Launching missiles over the horizon at a ship this deep in the atmosphere was laughable. They might actually get so hot from the friction that they set themselves off, but he had four guns happy to assist. And the air slowed the missiles, not the beams.

Good enough.

Phil went back to Fleet Centurion mode and studied the planet. Kremlin there. Not below him directly, but probably enough to take a shot at the ships overhead.

Again, part of the reason *CS-405* was here. Keep the bad guys occupied, while *Persephone* went for the kill. Phil had the shields and armor to resist something like that, although the lower he went, the cleaner a beam would be from the ground.

Still, in for a penny. In for a pound.

"Pilot, come starboard at this altitude and begin to put us overhead of the kremlin on the ground, but closer to the station we've been poking than to the others."

Here. Let me entice you to fire more missiles this way. And maybe get the guy on the ground to try a shot at us. A Type-4 would hurt, but he can't have that many, and we're moving and jamming.

Phil checked. Yes, Evan had the rear sensor array blasting the ground with what looked to be old television sitcoms, with enough power behind them that the wires of the buildings below might be playing the theme song all by themselves.

Phil wondered if that constituted a war crime, and laughed to himself. He had done meaner things to less deserving people in his time.

One shot of lightning flashed through the atmosphere as he watched.

Sure enough, ground fire, but damn, that was barely close enough to even count.

Still, that meant he had their attention.

"West, begin evasive maneuvering," Phil ordered. "Stay over this guy and within a big box as we circle overhead. At least until Veitengruber reports in."

"Aye aye, sir," the pilot replied.

Phil checked all his screens, but everything was within the range of outcomes they had gamed out. Not perfectly good, but not perfectly bad, either.

Now they just had to shut up the loudmouth on the ground.

THE RESCUE (FEBRUARY 17, 403)

GRANVILLE WATCHED as Admiral Kosnett's guns cleared the skies overhead of threats. At least any that seemed to have a chance of getting close.

"Stand by for maneuvering," he said, pitching the ship's nose down and pushing more power to the engines.

Time to play a game of tag.

Shields had been rebuilt from the glancing blow. All the paint was probably scorched off a rear quarter of the ship, but it hadn't penetrated. And the fuses had blown before it could overload everything.

He could live without life support right now. And the grav-plates were normally a heavy load on the generators, so he had extra power for shields and guns with them off, this deep in the atmosphere.

The ground kremlin vanished below the horizon as the altitude indicator decreased at almost the same rate as the airspeed indicator climbed. They surely knew he was there, but *Persephone* was moving at several times the speed of sound, right now.

"Overwatch, please provide a scan of the defensive arrays," Granville said into the radio.

Evan was watching the ground below for him. Granville needed to know what their capabilities were.

A file appeared in the inbox. Granville opened it as the autopilot took over. They were headed almost due west, relative, on this planet, and low enough that the sun would rise in another hour, if they maintained this course and heading.

Stupid, bordering on suicidal, but something he had always wanted to do, from low enough that you had a reverse sunrise. From orbit didn't count, when you might have one every couple of hours.

The fortress was laid out in a hexagon. Six walls protecting six towers, with a moat all the way around. From the looks of it, someone had turned a peninsula into an island by trenching a canal across the base. Radar scan said the depth of the water was five meters all the way around, so Granville assumed the whole thing was artificial. Maybe they built the island and then opened a channel to the river nearby, once all the concrete had hardened and started to cure.

Certainly, men on the ground with iron age technology were not going to be a threat.

Granville flashed back to the video he had watched. The interview with Lan and Kiel, when the man had first mentioned this planet.

What had he said?

Twenty-five years ago, give or take, Lan had been part

of a crew that delivered tractor parts, because the original load from a generation earlier had finally worn out, and there were no factories allowed here to make new parts.

So at best an early industrial civilization probably was allowed to exist, and nothing better. Certainly nothing high enough to threaten fifteen-meter-tall walls that looked eight meters thick at the base.

Each tower had a weapon mount, but the only fire directed at *CS-405* had come from inside the walls.

There. That looked like a gun battery on one side of a quad, with a landing field, a barracks, and probably the main building for the camp commandant and his staff. Buildings around the inside of the walls suggested the wall itself was solid, and those six turrets were probably anti-tank weapons designed to kill anything that a prisoner revolt might cook up.

He wasn't sure if they could knock down a police cutter or not, but the big gun certainly could, and the landing field had a couple of what looked like armed repulsor transports.

Just the sort of thing to go raid a prisoner's camp or city outside the walls, if you wanted to. Again, probably a threat to *Persephone*, if he decided to let them engage.

Quickly, he sent the map to the three gun stations, and programmed the course he wanted and locked it in. Rather than give too much away, he could come in at fifteen hundred meters, and then start to drop down when he was one hundred kilometers out. At this speed, the fortress would be four seconds away.

"Bow gun, concentrate on the orbital battery," he said. "Morgan and Spier, you have the landing field. We will overfly the fortress at transonic speed, at a very low altitude, so program your guns and let them handle the timing. We will be at Mach Two and nine hundred meters at the end, passing just right of center so that our centerline hits the landers. Questions?"

"What do you want killed after the primary targets?" Spier fired back.

He laughed out loud. Another one who understood audacity.

"Anything that moves, Gunner," Granville said. "The six turrets might be able to hurt us, so pour fire into them if you can."

"Splatter city, coming up," she laughed back.

Yes, he had the crew he needed to do this.

Granville looked down as he engaged the final pass in the autopilot and marveled. His hands were completely steady. He listened to his heart. All the mad adrenaline was burned out, leaving only a hard, steady beat.

He had been into the fire. Fought the dragon. Emerged successful.

"All hands, prepare to unleash hell," he said in a cheerful voice. "Four seconds to contact."

He held his hands over the controls, in case something went wrong, but Granville wasn't sure what he might do. At this speed, he would hit the ground before he even knew anything was wrong.

And today was not allowed to be his day to die.

The Type-3 in the bow opened up at fifty kilometers. Long, but just right to recycle for a second shot at close enough to pee on them as he flew by. Morgan and Spier waited, and then fired within a sixteenth note of each other, just before the bow gun fired a second round.

Persephone blasted through a cloud of smoke and fire, probably snuffing some fires like birthday candles. Granville watched more explosions in his rear cameras for a second, before he was too far away to make out details.

"*CS-405*, this is *Persephone*," he said in a calm voice. "First strafing run complete. Could we get a damage report, please?"

Chuckles came over the radio as Evan opened a line.

"Stand by," the Science Officer said.

Images from orbit appeared on Granville's screen. At least one of the two transports had been shattered, like an apple hit with a pulse pistol. The building housing the orbital gun had apparently also taken damage.

Good enough.

Granville brought the nose of his stallion around so he could line up a second shot. He could do this all day.

"*Persephone*, this is Kosnett," the Admiral's voice suddenly filled his ears. "Defending forces have surrendered. Repeat, defenders have struck their colors. Cease all combat operations while we sort out terms."

"Roger that," Granville replied.

Rather than just orbit, he looked for a spot where he could land. Someplace with good fields of fire and sky so nobody could sneak up on him. Preferably close to one of the villages he had seen on Evan's maps.

There. Low, rolling hill with nothing on top of it, overlooking a village on a tributary creek to the big river.

He dialed back the engines and slowed with a few hard waggles to bleed off speed. As he went overhead on a downwind, *Persephone* was only one hundred meters up and flying no faster than a skycar.

The hill he wanted didn't have any buildings on it, but it did have a small herd of cattle milling about.

He laughed over the intercom as he buzzed them, using sound and size to drive them off to the right, so he had a clear zone at the peak.

"What's so funny, top?" Spier asked over the line.

"It's a cattle ranch, Sailor," he chuckled some more as the landing skids deployed and he began to hover down to earth. "I've come home."

FAIRY GODMOTHER (FEBRUARY 19, 403)

"Technically, you are supposed to stay on the ship, Sam," Andre groused, watching the various panels he had insisted that the engineers add to the command centurion's station.

To hell with sitting around, just looking pretty, while the others did the work.

"Ah, but I'm only the Chief Medical Officer, Director," she smiled sweetly back at him, just to rub it in. "My place is down on the ground, tending to the injured and helping organize the evacuation."

Andre scowled at her, but the woman was immune. Worse, she had already reminded him twice that the Hippocratic Oath was on her side here.

Grumble.

"And being close to Trinidad has nothing to do with it, right?" Andre fired the last arrow in his quiver.

It was a solid hit. She blushed to the tips of her ears and the edge of her tunic.

"I have no idea what you're talking about, Director Gave," she said awkwardly after a moment.

Uh huh. Want to sell me a bridge, while we're at it?

Fine.

"Permission granted," Andre finally said.

He did have the legal authority to order the woman to remain aboard *Forgotten Mercy*, while her doctors went down in the hospital ship and treated the prisoners Veitengruber and his crew had rescued.

He would, however, lose all moral authority the moment he did so.

And she knew it.

Damn it.

"*Stunt Dude*, this is the bridge," Andre grumbled into the ship's comm. Somewhere aft, the monstrous LanderShip-sized beast was preparing to undock and begin the leisurely descent to the surface.

This war was over. For today.

"*Stunt Dude* here," Trinidad replied a moment later.

"Stand by for one additional passenger," Andre said, turning a sour scowl on one Dr. Sam Au, medical professional with the charming smile.

"Roger that," *Stunt Dude* said. "Who's coming?"

"Sam's joining you," Andre said, trying to sound professional and all that.

"Really?" the Dragoon said in a voice of barely-disguised glee. "Not a problem."

Andre hadn't thought it would be.

Those two had kept everything above-board for the entire mission. She was still technically a prisoner and he was her jailer. Those dinners together had been surrounded by significant numbers of salacious crew with watching eyes.

Hell, if anything, all the gossiping back and forth had done more to weld the two sides into a single, working whole than anything anybody might have recommended.

And Trinidad and Sam had never even so much as held hands. Someone would have noticed.

Still, everyone had noticed.

Sam's blush doubled again as Andre turned his attention to her.

"Godspeed, Doctor," he said drolly, but she was already headed to the hatch at a speed somewhere between a skip and a sprint.

Andre looked down from his momentous throne and found Ross smiling up at him. Andre was pretty sure that the woman who had accompanied them to the surface back at *Lighthouse Station* had been replaced by a doppelgänger version of his Flight Deck Advocate. Maybe yet another fairy godmother watching over star-crossed lovers.

Or something like that.

"Make sure they hold until their passenger is aboard," Andre ordered in an off-hand voice. "And then notify the flagship."

"Yes, Director Gave," she grinned.

Andre leaned back in his chair and considered things. They were just about six weeks out from the first anniversary of the meltdown on *CS-405* that had set this adventure in motion. If his CMO and her staff spent a week on the surface tending to serious cases, and then

then squadron made good time home, they could probably make it to *Osynth B'Udan* in that time.

Give it another four to six weeks, depending on the speed of bureaucracy, and the romance on the medical deck would either turn bittersweet, or completely insane.

"What's the betting on the outcome?" he asked her.

Andre found it telling that she raised one hand, palm down, and waggled it from side to side.

Fifty/fifty, but hey, look at the odds these crews had overcome so far.

ACTING FLEET CENTURION
(FEBRUARY 20, 403)

Heather and Siobhan had both nearly pitched a fit, but in the end, Phil was the commander around here, and he was allowed to pull rank. Even on *Lady Blackbeard* and *Ground Control*. And three days had been long enough for the various teams on the ground to sort things out.

Phil wanted to do this himself. There would never be another day like this.

He looked out the window as his shuttle came in to land. Unlike most flights, he was up in the cockpit in the co-pilot's seat, rather than aft in the crew compartment. He wanted to see this place with his own eyes, rather than just on a screen as they overflew.

And he had already ordered a lazy approach.

Stunt Dude's expanded marine force had come down with the LanderShip and spiked all the remaining guns in the kremlin with high explosives. They would have gone after the walls next, probably with a Type-3 beam, if Phil hadn't put his foot down.

The squadron was still deep behind enemy lines. Still at significant risk, especially with both *Persephone* and *Queen Anne's Revenge* on the surface. Time was most assuredly of the essence.

At least this wasn't a thriving colony he was about to upend, the planet five hundred meters beneath him. Trinidad had confirmed that there were no females at all on the surface, save for those in the surrendered garrison, and the Dragoon had rounded them all up and kept them safe from retribution.

One thousand, six hundred and fourteen men. Three of them admirals. One hundred twenty-nine naval captains. Most of the rest were officers of some type, many of them fliers like Veitengruber who had been lost on various missions over the years. Records showed eight thousand more, buried with whatever honors the men could arrange, in one of several cemeteries, at least until their remains could be repatriated. Not Phil's job today, but certainly something for someday.

They had even located one man who had served on *C-4268*, the vessel that had provided the stern section for *Persephone*. An actual, living representative of the Seventeenth Imperial Police Protectorate. Another one, since Veitengruber and his current crew had added that patch to their uniforms in a highly irregular breach of regulations that nobody was ever going to notice.

Many of the prisoners were aboard the hospital ship, seeing their first clinic in perhaps generations. There had been doctors gulaged here, but never any advanced medicines or equipment to take care of the locals.

The prisoners of *Buran* worked, or starved. If they died of exhaustion, that was just bad luck.

Which was why the garrison was safely kept away from the prisoners. Phil could trust his marines and crew not to do anything permanent to folks under their care.

Permanent being the operative term.

And the crew of seven orbital stations were down here, too, trying to come to grips with their own apocalypse, but at least they had survived.

Phil would have happily let Galin build a tugboat. There were four old light cruisers, seventeen destroyers, and eleven frigates in local orbit that could be used for parts, if someone had enough resources.

And anger.

Again, not his responsibility. He just had to get these people home.

The shuttle grounded with a whisper-soft touch. His people had been getting a lot more experience flying shuttles between ships and down to surfaces than they used to.

Phil smiled and unbuckled, rising and exiting with a nod of thanks to his pilot.

Outside, two lines of men had been drawn up as representatives of the rest. As formal as things could be done on a frontier world like this.

Phil emerged and walked over to where Centurion Granville Veitengruber, *RAN* and Imperial Officer and Gentleman, waited at the end of a line. He stopped and saluted the man. So much of this was only possible because of Veitengruber.

Phil was wearing his dress uniform for today. Nobody

down here had anything remotely like it, but the ragged men around him were crisp and proud, standing erect with tears flowing.

Veitengruber returned the salute with tears in his eyes, but that was acceptable. He had come out of his own personal hell, and then gone back in to save others.

How many of the men they would be able to save wouldn't have lasted another year or however long it took for someone to scrape together a war fleet for a task so mundane?

Doctor Au, the Chief Medical Officer of *Forgotten Mercy* was next in line, still dressed in her surgical scrubs. This set had blood splatters in a few places, so she had been working as well, and not just supervising the rescue of her mortal enemies.

She had a tired smile for Phil, but that was from her working so hard. And perhaps an approaching sunset, as reported by Yeoman Nakisha Onks.

The next man in line wasn't one Phil knew. The stranger was tall and lean. In his seventies, from the look of him. Ragged, like so many of them, and malnourished enough to be probably ten kilos lighter than he should have been, but all his teeth were there when he smiled, and his carriage was still firm and stubborn. Like Veitengruber, the man was crying.

Phil drew himself up as formally as he could and saluted him. This was a mere formality in many ways, but something that none of the men on the surface probably ever imagined would happen.

That the cavalry would actually come over the hill to rescue them.

"Admiral of the Red Carlyle Gustavsson, I relieve you," Phil boomed in a voice loud enough that everyone could hear. "*Mansi Detachment* of the *Fribourg Fleet* is ordered home."

"I stand relieved," the man replied in a voice barely above a whisper.

A ragged cheer broke out among the twenty men drawn up, and the one woman as well.

Phil found himself mobbed by total strangers who wanted to touch him, or salute him, or just smile. Their war was over, and many of them would get to die at home in bed.

Technically, the crew of a C-class hull was generally around forty men in active service, but Granville had only accepted a few of the many volunteers, once Admiral Kosnett had gotten everyone sorted into medical transportees and able-bodied crew he could add to existing vessels.

Granville already had a crew. An extra special one once Deni came aboard.

Still, they had a long sail ahead of them, so he had taken on six more engineers, four of whom had served as Chief Engineers on frigates or larger vessels before their capture. In addition, six more gunners were aboard, to provide crews and support for the three he had.

Only two additional bridge crew had made the cut, of all those commanders and officers who had inquired.

Manning the communications and sensors console today was forty-six-year-old Petty Officer, Third Class Anders Waktcomm, the only known survivor of *C-4268,* taken twenty-one years ago at *Englonn* while on customs patrol and never heard from again.

Granville had gotten some of the stories, but apparently most of the men on this planet were either commanding officers that had needed to be separated from other crew that they might rally, or troublemakers where it was easier to dump them here, while the *Fribourg Empire* might have executed them if the situations were reversed.

Waktcomm had been in the latter category, causing mischief gladly and with revelry at all the places he had been sent, until they finally put him here as the only place left he wouldn't set fires or sabotage power systems. A man who had never, ever given up the war.

The other man, seated carefully in the pilot's seat but not touching anything, wasn't really flying the ship. Not yet, anyway. Liftoff of a slightly-damaged and beat-to-hell police cutter from a planetary surface required more experience, so Granville had handled that task himself. The commander's chair was already set up for him to fly, so it hadn't changed anything from the last several times he had flown *Persephone* to orbit.

But Granville couldn't think of a better place for Admiral Gustavsson to be, than on the bridge of the only true Imperial warship in this squadron, as they started the sail home to Imperial space.

Going home.

On the screens, the sky finally grew dark as they broke through the atmosphere and made it into space. Granville turned the bow to the east as they did, looping out and over as he inserted the vessel into orbit.

It was safe today. Admiral Kosnett and *Lady Blackbeard* had spiked all the other stations with weapons fire once the crews had abandoned ship. Over the next year or three, big pieces would be falling from orbit, but most of them would burn up, and the only people at risk on the ground below were the crews of the stations and the kremlin itself.

Granville really couldn't find any sympathy for those people. He tried. Prayed and meditated on his luck, his faith, and his destiny, but those bastards deserved whatever they got. Even Deni agreed on that point.

On the scanners, everyone was already in place. *CS-405* rode in high orbit, protecting the squadron from harm. *Packmule* led *Forgotten Mercy* in a lower orbit, with *Queen Anne's Revenge* sitting on an escorting flank.

He checked once more, but nothing had changed. Siobhan and Heather had calculated the first layover and rechecked their numbers. *Persephone* could actually make it home long before everyone else, simply by not dropping out into RealSpace and making a straight run.

Granville had even considered it, for all of about two seconds. While he wanted to be home, this meant to much too the men and women with him. To all the ex-prisoners having their first taste of freedom in far too long. They would go home as a single squadron, comprised of probably the most motley collection of stolen ships ever put together.

It was when they got there that Granville planned to have a nasty argument with whatever admiral was in charge, or the governor. He knew Imperial officers, having been one. And bureaucrats.

Those people would never simply consent to sending the hospital ship home, possibly without express orders from either Grand Admiral Wachturm, the old Red Admiral of legend, or Fleet Centurion Jessica Keller, the new Red Admiral in command of this entire theater. Or Her Imperial Majesty Karl VIII.

It might take an act of piracy to free them. And another to send Lan and Kiel home.

Good thing Granville knew where he could locate some pirates in a pinch.

"What's so funny?" Admiral Gustavsson asked, having turned to look and caught the grin on Granville's face.

"Thinking about explaining all this to the Fleet Admiral on station when we get home, sir," Granville replied, unable yet to suppress his mirth. "And what we might have to do to convince them to send *Buran*'s people home. Our last year has been one long act of piracy, and we might not be done."

"In that case, sign me up, Veitengruber," Gustavsson smiled back. "Without your pirates, we would have probably died there and been forgotten. Whatever you need, you have but to ask."

"All I ever wanted to do was serve, Admiral," Granville said.

There wasn't anything for the man to say, so he just nodded and turned back to his own console. Granville hadn't explained, to him or any of the rescuees, that he and Deni would not be welcomed back together.

Without Deni, he wasn't going to return. If *Aquitaine* wouldn't take him, some pirates somewhere would.

"*Persephone*, this is Kosnett," the other Admiral's voice came over the line. "What is your status?"

Granville checked before answering, something that had been pounded into him so deep it would never wash out.

"All systems nominal, Flag," Granville replied, feeling the words settle him.

Galin had come over and helped Isiah and Arla take the life support systems apart, with the assistance of a dozen experts on Imperial engineering to help. It was running better now than it ever had, but Granville was still going to add a greenhouse room back in frame two, near the primary air intakes, once he got home and had the time. The air remained a little stinky, even after the work, and he wanted to smell dirt and flowers, even in space.

"Roger that, *Persephone*," Kosnett said. "You have the flag."

Granville felt the tears well up again. That had happened a lot lately, and probably wasn't going to get better anytime soon. That was okay. He had Deni, and his freedom.

Next came the future.

Until this moment, he hadn't really believed they could do it. He had kept expecting something to fail. That other shoe to drop.

Granville closed the line so he could speak on just the intercom for a moment.

"Admiral Gustavsson, would you like to do the honors, sir?" he asked.

Both men in the forward seats turned to look back,

mirroring each other in their tears. The Admiral nodded after a moment.

"Push the blue button on the top right to open the general comm," Granville said. "And then the green button when you're ready to make the Jump."

"Thank you," Gustavsson said quietly.

"Squadron, this is Admiral Gustavsson, aboard *IFV Persephone*," he said, his voice growing in power and gravity as he found his own belief. "I have the flag. All vessels ahead standard and prepare for JumpSpace. We will rendezvous at Waypoint One. Thank you, and Godspeed."

IFV Persephone leapt into the darkness.

VALIANT (APRIL 2, 403)

It had been one hell of a crazy year.

Phil had built slack into the run home, just so they could do this, even after something broke on *Persephone* and they lost a day getting the primary reactors back online. Plus the time necessary to shift megatons of food from *Packmule* to *Forgotten Mercy*, in order to feed two thousand extra hands on the long sail. But if it had taken too much longer, Phil had considered raiding a few planets on the way home, just to stock the pantry one last time.

And to remind *Buran* that there were pirates loose in *Trusski*'s sector, too.

But they were here. He was, anyway. The rest of the squadron was out in deep space, hiding from anyone who might shoot first and ask questions later. Especially with vessels that belonged to *The Holding*, or had at least been designed and built by those folks.

Technically, all of them belonged to the *Republic*. The Senate had specific rules for capturing non-neutral, civilian warships in warzones, and this was a Republic formation, regardless of the flag of convenience. Had all those ships been sold, Phil's share as Command Centurion would have made him phenomenally wealthy, and most of his crew would have at least a year's salary deposited in their accounts.

But only *Packmule* would be auctioned. *Persephone* would be returned to service with the *Fribourg Fleet*, although he had no idea if they would keep her, strike her, or turn her into a museum exhibit. Didn't matter. She had served well.

The other two ships would be sent home. Well, *Forgotten Mercy* would be, period. He would only let them keep that ship over his dead body. And if necessary, Phil would order *Queen Anne's Revenge* sold, and then turn over the funds to Lan and Kiel, along with his own money, and probably a big chunk of capital volunteered from his crews, to buy them something new.

None of this would have been possible, but for their assistance.

"All hands, sixty seconds to emergence," Evan's voice roused him.

CS-405's bridge had been cleaned and painted on the way home. Having an overfull crew of willing workers helped. Phil was in the dress uniform today. He could have done this in his regular uniform, but damn it, this should be special.

Apparently, the whole bridge crew had come to the same conclusion, because everyone was dressed up today, even though he hadn't ordered it.

The man seated next to Evan, in the chair Siobhan

would have normally sat, didn't have a proper dress uniform, but they had managed to work something up in red that was close enough.

Phil took one last look around the bridge as they made their final approach, knowing that things were going to change soon.

Emergence.

CS-405 dropped into RealSpace clear out on the edge of good navigation from *Osynth B'Udan*'s gravity well. Out where the big freighters that maneuvered like comets would come in, so they could safely waddle down to a closer orbit, without much risk of hitting anyone on the way.

"*Osynth B'Udan* Flight Control, this is Command Centurion Phil Kosnett aboard *RAN CS-405*, flying an Imperial Flag as part of Keller's squadron," he said formally. The signal would take thirty seconds to even arrive down there. "Requesting an escort with a senior officer aboard. Reply on this channel, please."

And there it was. Depending on who was on duty down there right now, they might roll out the red carpet, and they might scramble all squadrons. Creator only knew what news Phil had missed in the last year.

Especially considering what the last five years had been like around here.

"Evan, maintain full shields, but leave the gun crews on standby," Phil ordered.

They weren't in battle, and hopefully weren't about to be, but Brinich was prepared to take over Tactical duties if something went wrong.

"Aye aye, sir," the Tactical/Science Officer replied crisply.

They were broadcasting their transponder loud enough that damned near anybody in the system was going to know they were here, but Phil knew that Evan's hand was poised over the button to drop them back into Jump at the slightest hint that the political tides had turned around here.

Who knew if Karl VIII was still on the throne, or if another pretender had come along and rallied enough of the nobles to do something about it? Or if Keller being in charge had finally pushed enough of the old farts in admiral's uniforms over some metaphorical edge.

Phil didn't see a man like Emmerich Wachturm rolling over easily, but they might be in the middle of an Imperial civil war right now, too.

A little console light went on, letting him know that the message had at last crossed the orbit of the planet below, so it was time to start expecting company. Based on First Expeditionary Fleet, that would be about five minutes at a dead minimum, but he didn't see the Imperials being that much on the ball, even in a frontier town like *Osynth B'Udan*.

So Phil was surprised as hell when the scanners lit up at five minutes, fifteen seconds with a massive, overlapping ripple of emergence signatures.

Someone had just dropped an entire task force in his lap.

"We're being hailed," Evan said rather offhandedly after a second.

"I'll take it on my personal console for now," Phil said.

Might as well preserve the surprise as long as possible.

"*CS-405*, this is *IFV Valiant*, Tom Provst commanding," a dark, heavy voice came over the line and Phil's personal screen lit up with a stranger in red.

Phil had never met Provst, but the man was famous, even in the Republic. Captain of the original battleship *Blackbird* at the famous battle known as *Third Iger*. One of Wachturm's top students, the man had been left in overall command of the entire fleet, functionally the entire Empire, when Wachturm went to retrieve Centurion Wiegand and turn her into an Emperor.

And Phil knew what *Valiant* was. Hell, he had spent a year escorting the class ship, this vessel's older sister, with Jessica aboard and Denis in command.

RAN Vanguard.

From the Jump signatures, there were four cruisers around him as well. None of them quite the size of *VI Victrix*, but the CEE design was still a powerful, monstrous beast capable of taking apart any battlecruiser of the previous generation.

Seven corvettes were there as well, in a shell outside the cruisers, protecting them in case this was a trap and someone was about land on their backs. *Persephone* might be willing to try, but Phil doubted that even Veitengruber's heart was enough to take on a modern corvette, let alone a squadron of them.

Not that the man wouldn't have tried, if Phil had called on him to do so.

Granville Veitengruber might be one of theirs by original commission, but Phil was going to ask First Lord to move heaven and earth to keep him in green and black.

"*Valiant*, this is Kosnett," he said. "We got separated from *Vanguard* after the raid on *Severnaya Zemlya* when both JumpSails were lost. In the process of limping home, we decided to turn ourselves into pirates and have a variety of adventures across *Altai* sector. Might have made it here two days ago, but this was too good of an anniversary to miss."

"That would explain a few things that Imperial Intelligence shrugged at," Provst said. "Their whole frontier got soft, all of a sudden. Were they chasing you?"

"Most likely," Phil said. "We attacked *Barnaul, Laptev, Abakn, Kyzyl,* and *Mansi* on our way home."

"You're just a scout corvette, Kosnett," Provst's voice turned questioning. "How did you attack planets?"

Phil figured there were enough beams centered on his ship right now to carve it into rabbit-sized pieces, because nobody could explain something like that. They would be presuming he had been captured and turned, and was trying to open the gates for barbarians to flood in.

Hell, he would, in their shoes.

"That's why I came in alone first, *Vanguard*," Phil felt the smile take hold of his face. "The rest of my task force is parked out in deep space, waiting for you to come and escort them safely home."

"Task force?"

Now the confusion had set in.

After all, the least of Jessica Keller's warships was hardly a threat to anything, especially not a bigger Hammerhead, to say nothing of a Mako.

Or any of the vessels currently surrounding him with big guns.

"Told you we stopped and raided several places along the way, *Valiant*," Phil said. "My crew also captured four enemy vessels and pressed them into service."

"You did what?" Provst asked, his face on the tiny screen utterly shocked now. "How?"

"We're the *Republic of Aquitaine* Navy, Provst," Phil smiled proudly. "That's what we do."

Yeah, play *that* back at my Court Martial. I bloody well dare you.

"So what proof do you have that I should believe you, *CS-405*?" Provst growled.

As if a full task force of Bedrov-designed warships was at risk. Add First Expeditionary to the mix, and they might be able to sweep *Samara*'s skies clean of *Buran*'s fleet for the first time in two generations.

"The best one imaginable, *Vanguard*," Phil said with a smile.

He clicked a button and the image of Tom Provst appeared on the big screen at the far end of the room. At the same time, the camera image over on that Heavy Dreadnaught would shift from just showing Phil Kosnett to letting Provst see the entire bridge of *CS-405*.

"Admiral?" Phil said quietly.

He smiled when the older man unbuckled from his seat and rose. Provst's eyes suddenly shifted down from Phil's face and locked on the man.

"My God," Provst gasped in surprise. "Carlyle?"

"Hello, Tom," Admiral Gustavsson said in a surprisingly strong voice. "We have a fantastic story to tell you, but first, I need you to help me bring home the rest of my men, and then make sure everyone else has a chance to make it home as well."

"How…?" Provst asked.

"We located and liberated a prison planet in *Altai* sector, *Vanguard*," Phil said. "We brought them all home, but my mission is not yet complete."

REVOLUTIONARY (APRIL 10, 403)

He would miss this, but Andre Gave, Brevet Command Centurion in command of *RAN Forgotten Mercy*, would never let the folks back home know the truth. He would miss this bridge, and these people.

Not the half-dozen Imperial Marines in partial armor and their attitude problems, surrounding everyone on his bridge, but the other folks. Kav, the mousy woman in charge of security. Po, his comms officer. Gan, handling Sciences. Ross, Flight Deck Boss.

But mostly Wil. The man had come a long ways from addressing him relentlessly as "Your Grace" at the beginning to where they were today, parked at a major Imperial Starbase, getting ready to offload the last of the *RAN* folks.

In a few minutes, only the original crew and a team from the Imperial Navy would be aboard her, as the ship sailed slowly and majestically out to the edge of the gravity well, waved once, and started the long run home.

"Sir? Are you sure?" one of the marines spoke up from his spot. "My orders allow some leeway here if you wanted it."

Andre fixed the man with a harsh glare. Even the marine was smart enough to shut up at that point and fall into parade rest, eyes fixed on some distant horizon, rather than press his luck any further.

Not that Andre would have ripped him apart verbally in front of this crew, but he might have decided to ask Phil to pick a fight on the topic with Grand Poobah Provst next week. And Phil owed him at least a few.

Andre rose from the Director's chair with something approximating dignity. At least as much as he could muster, given who he was most days.

He had worn his dress uniform today, broken out specifically for the task. Nothing less would do. A clock on the wall marked the apocalypse.

"Wil," Andre said in a heavy, sad voice. "It's time."

Wil rose from the pilot's station as though he was in pain. The man was small in stature normally, but today he seemed almost shrunken in on himself.

Fear of the future, perhaps. Of how his overlords would interpret the entire charade in the light of hindsight.

Provst had flatly refused to accept any claims of asylum, right up front. Not that Andre could blame the man. Provst was an old school, biblical patriarch these days, to look at him.

Fire and death and brimstone cast as flesh.

But he had also made it easy enough to save all this

crew the agony of deciding whether they should attempt to flee to a better world, or return to *Buran*.

Wil stepped away from his station and approached Andre with a slow, measured tread, as though he was walking to his own hanging. It was a feeling Andre understood quite well, having felt the same way himself, once upon a time.

Andre rose as Wil got close. Took the man's measure from the precise two steps away. Watched Wil draw a breath in, that seemed to inflate him into a human again, and perhaps a shade larger.

That, my friend, is what command will do to you. You fight it as much and as long as you can, but at some point, you must face up to your fears and overcome them.

And yet, Andre looked forward to this crew returning home. After so long with him in command, the next person would be in for a raft of comic insubordination if they tried to crack the whip on a crew that had served under Andre Gave, Ethical Philosopher and Revolutionary.

"Brevet Command Centurion Andre Gave, I relieve you," Wil said, raising his right fist to cover his heart.

It helped that Wil was crying, so Andre didn't feel so bad about his own tears. Glancing around, so was everyone else.

"Director Ko Namas Allon Wil, I stand relieved," Andre returned the salute. "You will take command of this vessel, subject to the normal rules and regulations, where you will exercise excellence and demand the same of your crew, that the whole reflect the greatest acclaim in serving the needs of the entire ethical peoples of this galaxy."

Not quite the oath by which a Republic Centurion was charged with command, but close enough. They weren't serving the Republic and the Senate, but by all that was holy they would certainly infect the rest of *The Holding* with a different understanding of ethical behavior.

Assuming that stupid God of theirs didn't order the entire crew executed or put on a prison planet for not having resisted crazed, violent pirates more forcefully. Or something equally ludicrous.

But that was tomorrow's problem. Right now, they needed his help getting home.

Andre stepped to one side as Wil moved to the Director's chair and sat. Andre nodded to him, and to everyone else, and moved to the hatch, trailed by his two Imperial bodyguards he had been afraid would shower with him at one point, so close did they stick to him.

At the hatch, Wil called out one last time.

"Andre," he said quietly. "I'll do you proud."

"You already have, my friend," Andre grinned back at him as the hatch opened and he stepped into eternity. "You already have."

CHAPERONE (APRIL 10, 403)

They had known it was coming. Nothing but the most drastic actions on their parts could have prevented it, and neither of them were ready to leap off of a cliff.

Not yet.

Trinidad watched through a giant picture window as the soon-to-be-former *RAN Forgotten Mercy* was readied for her departure in two hours. The vessel had gone through a rapid dry-dock with every engineer available to help clean, tune, and fix things. It wasn't as good as new, but it was probably as close as it was ever going to get again.

For a moment, his old self surfaced, and he began placing cameras and Directors of Photography in his mind. Anything not to have to face this future.

But this was going to be a different kind of movie. Gone were the gonzo stunts and helmet cameras recording gunfights at odd angles and single takes. This would probably start with a tight focus, just to set the scene with our lovebirds, before slowly pulling back to an infinite horizon.

Endings.

A hand found his, took hold, squeezed it. Trinidad looked down at the sad smile on Sam's face. Very shortly, she would be boarding that ship in front of him, and the chances of him ever seeing her again they both knew were close enough to zero as to not matter counting. Roll the credits and understand that there wasn't a sequel coming.

She didn't speak now, just held his hand. Until the last month, even that much had been more than they had allowed themselves, surrounded constantly by two crews of watchful eyes.

Trinidad had gotten the distinct impression, from her people as well as his, that doing more than just holding hands would have been acceptable, at least in their eyes, but both of them would be returning home and facing some level of judicial inquiry into their actions over the last year. Best not to have to add crimes of the heart to the list.

A hand poked him on the back of the shoulder. His chaperone, the ghost who had been following them everywhere, just so Nakisha could report that nothing had ever crossed a line.

"Kiss her, damn it," Nakisha insisted. "I won't tell anyone, and you will live the rest of your life regretting it if you don't."

He glanced back, but the young marine's face was grim, almost insistent. Sam's face was serious.

He considered his marine. She was probably good for

her word on this one. They had been through too much together, not just in the last year, but in the last three.

Trinidad turned towards Sam and leaned forward, just a little.

Unsure.

Unwilling to cross a line uninvited, but Sam stepped slightly forward as well. Her hand found his side. Another went around his neck.

Perhaps an invitation.

He kissed her.

It was a first kiss, and a last kiss. At least as far as they knew. It might have lasted eternity, but he couldn't tell. He just wanted to revel in it while he could, knowing that the music was going to start swelling up at some point, an orchestral movement designed to flood the theater in tears before the credits rolled.

Eventually they broke the kiss. The hug lasted longer, but he finally stepped back, just so he could fix her smile and face in his memory.

Stunt Dude turned to his marine and nodded.

"You should escort her to the ship now, Marine," he ordered in a soft voice.

Sam nodded as well, understanding. She turned and bowed her head to the marine.

"Shall we, Nakisha?" Sam asked quietly.

Rather than wait and perhaps start crying, Sam walked towards the dock, looking back once to smile at him as she went down the hallway towards her ship.

Trinidad watched until the two women turned a corner and vanished from sight, then he turned and watched the final preparations as an Admiral of the Red aboard a refurbished police cutter prepared to escort the hospital ship to the first Jump.

He would wait here until it vanished from sight as well.

Only then could he return to his war.

PIRATES (APRIL 11, 403)

THE FORMER *RAN Forgotten Mercy* had made their first Jump away from *Osynth B'Udan*, presumably never to be seen again. Granville still had a mixed crew of extremely senior officers filling in junior slots, at least until Fleet sorted out what they wanted to do with this antique, recaptured hull.

And the man Phil Kosnett and Heather Lau had tapped to command her.

That would probably come up tomorrow, when he returned to station for what might be the last time, but Granville was *RAN* now. Oath and Hero, as several of his new comrades had reminded him.

His friends.

People willing to put their careers on the line to protect his, knowing that there were many ways someone like Admiral of the Red Tom Provst might handle this situation, some of which might get ugly.

Tomorrow's chore.

Tonight, he was off duty.

Admiral Gustavsson had the bridge, commanding this one tiny vessel as she made her slow and deliberate way back to the station, knowing that it might be the last time any of them ever served in space again, after so long as prisoners. The Admiral could go out in style.

Granville had Deni. And that was all that really mattered.

Their cabin was tiny. Bigger than any of his other crew had, but barely enough for the two of them, naval architects never having guessed that a man might bring his husband into space with him. Deni sat on the bunk and grinned with that impossible good humor that never left the man, even foaling horses in the worst storms imaginable.

Granville sat on the chair and just stared at him.

"You don't think he'll do it?" Deni asked. "Kosnett won't go toe to toe with that other admiral for you?"

"No, I think he will, my love," Granville said.

"So why are you so nervous then, Granvie?"

"What do we do next?" Granville despaired. "What happens if they order me back to duty and then Court Martial me?"

"Do you honestly think that all those other admirals and captains will stand for you being mistreated, you big goof?" Deni laughed. "After everything you did?"

Granville fell silent, almost like he'd been punched in the stomach. Would they?

Most of those men had been there so long that they might not even know Karl VII, let alone his Empire-saving daughter Karl VIII. But would they speak up to defend a man guilty of some of the worst social crimes recognized?

They might. Kosnett would. As would *Ground Control*, *Lady Blackbeard*, and *Stunt Dude*.

Why was he so frightened of tomorrow?

And then he understood, watching the merry twinkle in Deni's irrepressible eyes.

"So what do we do after the Navy is done with us?" Granville asked.

Deni's grin became almost impossibly wide.

"I am never riding a horse again," he stated categorically. "Never getting anywhere near a cow or ranch again, so help me God. I will divorce you if you make me."

Granville laughed and felt something finally break loose in his chest.

How long had he been waiting for the other shoe to drop? Months? Years? A lifetime of secrets ago?

He laughed until tears came. Deni as well.

"Better?" Deni asked after Granville finally got it more or less back together.

"Yes," Granville said. "I think I can do this."

"So do you want to stay in uniform with *Aquitaine*?" Deni's voice turned serious.

Granville shrugged.

"Short of getting transferred to some strange patrol vessel, I'm not sure I could go back to taking orders again," he decided. "Having *Persephone* was enough."

"Okay," Deni nodded. "I doubt if enough of *NovLao* survived the Beast to matter, at least at this point, so going there for our honeymoon is right out, unless Kosnett can talk his mythical dragon Keller into cutting *The Holding* in two for us. And *Aquitaine* is no more your home than mine, but it might be a good place to start. Plus, all our new friends keep talking about Keller's other people: *Corynthe*. Maybe you should go out there and get a job teaching those people how to be proper pirates. From what I've heard, they're junior varsity compared to the *RAN*."

"Don't let them hear you say that," Granville grinned. "They still duel with blades for that sort of insult."

"You don't think I could take them?" Deni puffed up with bravado.

"Oh, I'm sure you could," Granville laughed. "But then we'd probably turn into warlords or something after we embarrassed too many of them. They'd have to make us kings or something."

"Challenge Accepted. Granville Veitengruber," Deni's eyes lit up with fierce, merry daring.

"So what do we do for money?" Granville let pedestrian worries bubble up, with the big things seemingly settled.

"Demand back wages from the Emperor, plus hazard pay," Deni's laughter would not be denied. "Plus, you've been a Republican officer for a while, so they owe you money there. I've been a deck hound, so we'll throw that in there. And demand a share of money when they sell *Persephone*. According to rumor, the commander is due cash when they pay off a captured ship."

"You've given this too much thought," Granville accused him.

"I have had nothing else to occupy me," Deni turned

serious. "Except to worry about you every time you went out. Whether or not you'd come back to me."

"Always," Granville said. "I will never let anything keep us apart now. If I have to move Heaven and Empire to do it."

"Good," Deni said, turning and sliding into the bunk. "Let's go to bed and celebrate a new beginning."

Granville rose and touched the hull above him once for luck, a thing that every fighter pilot did when they were getting ready for combat.

Except his wars were done. *Persephone* had brought him and all the others home.

Now he could be free.

RESOLUTE (APRIL 12, 403)

LAN FOUND HIMSELF CRYING. But that was acceptable, as Kiel was, as well.

Director Kosnett appeared to be close to tears, as did *Ground Control* Lau, *Lady Blackbeard* Skokomish, and the indomitable *Stunt Dude*.

Lan turned his face away from his companions and stared through the big viewport at the tiny vessel, parked carefully near the dock in a slot that would have held *Packmule* comfortably.

He had spent enough years in space to understand that the tininess was only relative, at this distance. The ship was at least thirty percent again larger than *Resolute Revolution* had been. And brand new.

Director Kosnett had indeed been required to sell their old vessel, but the Imperial bureaucrat had not raised too much of a stink at the price demanded, which still appeared, at least to Lan, to have been utterly outrageous, for a battered freighter verging on three generations old.

But they had also appraised it purely on tonnage, and then counted it as a captured warship, because there was a stolen gun mounted on the front of the cargo deck. The price was good enough to replace *Resolute Revolution* with a bigger, better vessel. One that had two large cabins and four small ones, so he and Kiel could transport passengers between the stars, and not just tuna steaks.

And it contained that most magical of inventions, unknown back home: A JumpSail. Along with a complete set of spare parts and instructions, good enough to last them for probably twenty years without visiting an Imperial starport for repairs.

Not that Lan intended to wait that long.

"Beautiful," he murmured, feeling Kiel take his hand and squeeze it.

Director Kosnett had promised to *make them whole*. It was a legal term, and the vessel before them was half of that promise delivered. And as Lan watched, a small tug was slowly backing itself up to the aft ramp to deliver a load of cargo in standard shipping containers, homemade to *Holding* dimensions.

The two of them turned to the teary-eyed comrades of the last year, and the one fearsome man who was the terrible overlord of this station, Supreme Director Provst.

Kiel had always been the better communicator. It was why Lan let her negotiate deals.

But words failed them both, today.

"Thank you," she finally managed. "A year ago, we doubted."

"A year ago, so did I," Director Kosnett replied in just as emotional a voice. "But for your help, your understanding, none of this would have been possible. But for your standards, it would not have turned out the same."

"Our standards?" Lan asked.

The man nodded, at once crisp and fierce.

"At each station," Kosnett said, "at each decision, I was reminded that there were more options than simply violence. With Doctor Au, she finally became convinced that she might serve evil, simply by not questioning the will of a God, regardless of its orders. As one does not. Yours was the ethical standard that infected all of us, not to worship or fear that god, in turn, but to treat one another as humans, and to remember that our humanity stretched across the boundaries of culture that separate us. We retained the moral and ethical high ground by never ceding it. Never cutting corners and allowing our baser natures to run free. For that, I thank you. As does my crew."

Lan sniffled. As did Kiel. And several others. Even terrible Warlord Provst appeared moved to something approaching humanity at the words.

"And now?" Lan asked.

"Now you will return home," Admiral Provst said simply. "We have tuned your new vessel to the highest standards possible, and are loading it with cargo, but you will become the enemy again soon. My crew will board to fly you to the edge of the planetary system, and then debark so you can return to *Buran* space. I will not say you are welcome to return here, as I consider you enemies of my nation and my Emperor, but I will also issue instructions to the locals to treat you as a neutral vessel, if you call again. And I speak with the voice of the Grand Admiral himself, and Jessica Keller."

Lan supposed that would have to do. There were no other neutrals here at *Osynth B'Udan*, being a system almost as reinforced as *Samara* supposedly was, perhaps more so with this fierce man's force currently in residence, and facing *The Holding* across a hostile band of space.

And it was entirely possible that the Scholars would confiscate this vessel and its cargo when they returned to *Holding* space. If they did. Perhaps they would trade here as neutrals for a while.

He could only hope that the crew of the released medical cruiser, the former *RAN Forgotten Mercy*, would get home first, and explain everything well enough to whatever officious prick happened to be on duty when the vessel docked.

Lan bowed to the terrible Director as one would a Minister of the Eighth Rank. Formal and official. He felt Kiel do the same.

For Kosnett, the bow was deeper, and more heart-felt.

Who could have imagined?

"What will you call her?" Director Kosnett asked, curious.

Lan turned to Kiel and shared a wondrously evil smile.

"We had considered several names," Kiel answered with glee. "Things like *405*, or *Queen Anne's Revenge*, or perhaps even *Kosnett* were entirely inappropriate, to say nothing of the security troubles if we called it *Mansi*. In the end, one name struck us as the perfect way to remember our time with you, and the possibility of finding truth and honor among the barbarians. As we did with our friends."

"Indeed?" Kosnett's wry smile spoke volumes.

"Indeed," Kiel agreed. "We will call the vessel *Lighthouse*, for all the obvious as well as the subtle meanings that only those of us who were there would know."

Kosnett surprised them with a second bow, as deep as they had given him.

"I will let Bok and Avelina know," he said. "They will appreciate the joke."

Lan grinned at the thought of *Duke Avelina of Lighthouse*. The young woman was perfect for the role.

And perhaps someday, he would go and see if he could find the planet. Lan had no doubt that it had only temporarily been abandoned, and that Keller and Provst would likely return there.

He would remember to pack a case of good wine, and maybe a cargo hold filled with grapevines for planting.

That cowboy, Bok Battenhouse, would appreciate that.

READ MORE!

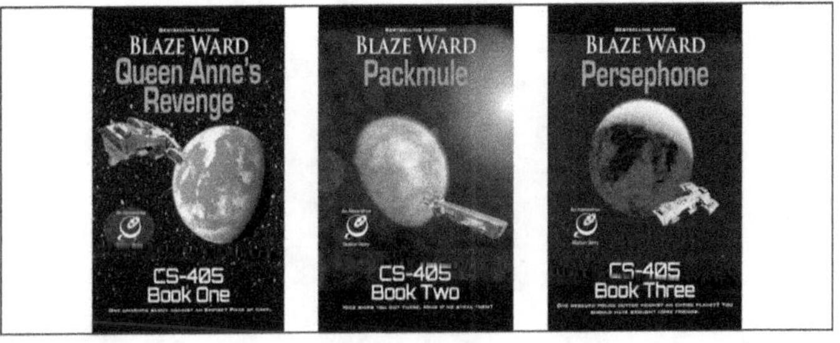

Be sure to read all three of the CS-405 books!
Queen Anne's Revenge
Packmule
Persephone
Available at your favorite retailers!

ABOUT THE AUTHOR

Blaze Ward writes science fiction in the Alexandria Station universe (Jessica Keller, The Science Officer, The Story Road, etc.) as well as several other science fiction universes, such as Star Dragon, the Collective, and more. He also writes odd bits of high fantasy with swords and orcs. In addition, he is the Editor and Publisher of *Boundary Shock Quarterly Magazine*. You can find out more at his website www.blazeward.com, as well as Facebook, Goodreads, and other places.

Blaze's works are available as ebooks, paper, and audio, and can be found at a variety of online vendors (Kobo, Amazon, and others). His newsletter comes out quarterly, and you can also follow his blog on his website. He really enjoys interacting with fans, and looks forward to any and all questions—even ones about his books!

Never miss a release!

If you'd like to be notified of new releases, sign up for my newsletter.

I will never spam you or use your email for nefarious purposes. You can also unsubscribe at any time.

http://www.blazeward.com/newsletter/

Connect with Blaze!

Web: www.blazeward.com
Boundary Shock Quarterly (BSQ):
https://www.boundaryshockquarterly.com/

facebook.com/KRPBlaze
goodreads.com/Blaze_Ward

ABOUT KNOTTED ROAD PRESS

Knotted Road Press fiction specializes in dynamic writing set in mysterious, exotic locations.

Knotted Road Press non-fiction publishes autobiographies, business books, cookbooks, and how-to books with unique voices.

Knotted Road Press creates DRM-free ebooks as well as high-quality print books for readers around the world.

With authors in a variety of genres including literary, poetry, mystery, fantasy, and science fiction, Knotted Road Press has something for everyone.

Knotted Road Press
www.KnottedRoadPress.com

www.ingramcontent.com/pod-product-compliance
Lightning Source LLC
Chambersburg PA
CBHW070643100726
47907CB00007B/2083